THE STANDARD

VERITAS NORMA SUI ET FALSI EST

Volume 1 / Number 1

2026

The Story Grid Universe

The Quest to Expand the Truth

Story Grid Writers' Mentorship

Story Grid Guild

STO
GR

Story Grid University

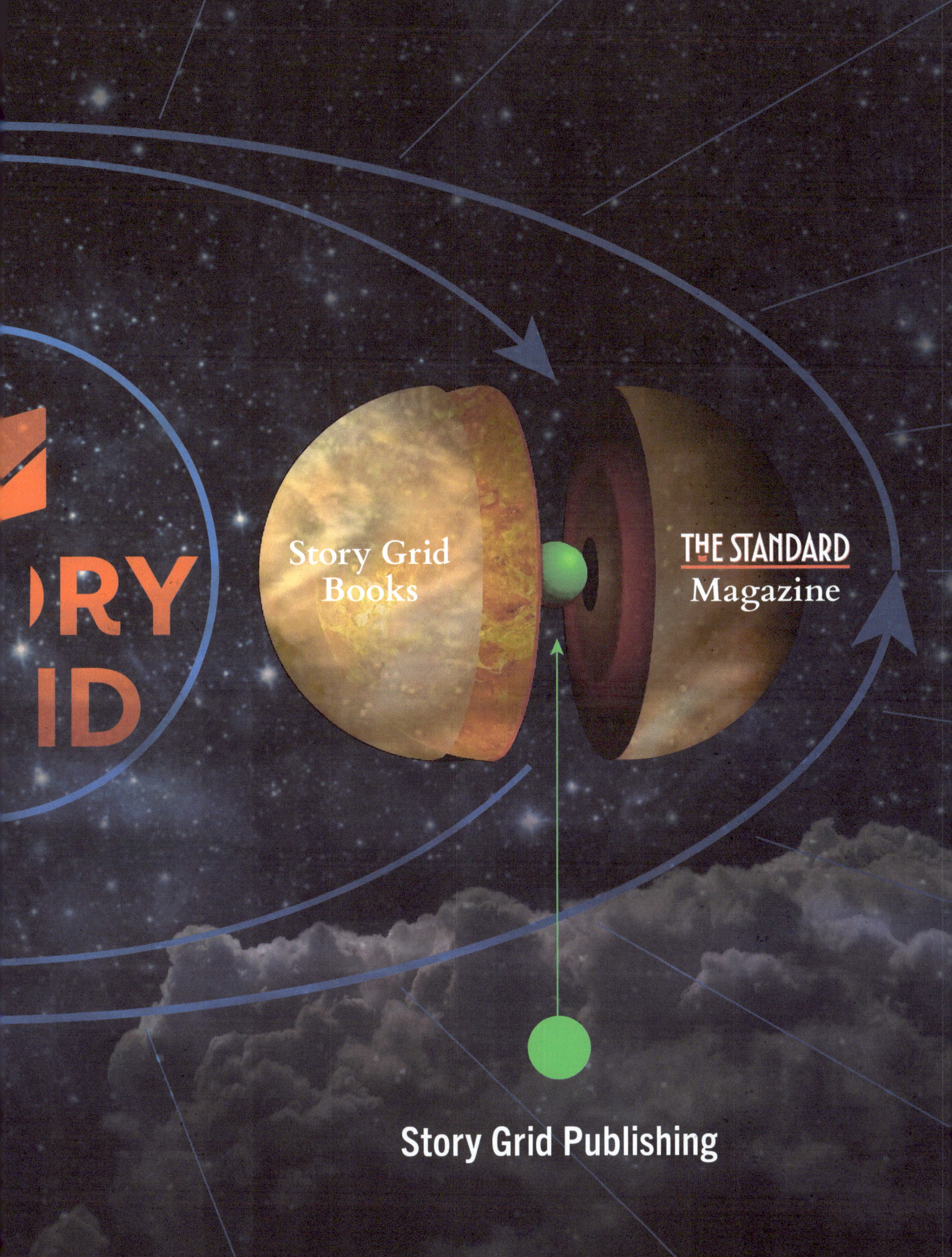

Story Grid
Books
THE STANDARD
Magazine
Story Grid Publishing

THE ST

VERITAS NORMA SUI ET FALSI EST

SPRING

Contents

Volume 1 / Number 1

2026

The Candymaker's Son. Page 15

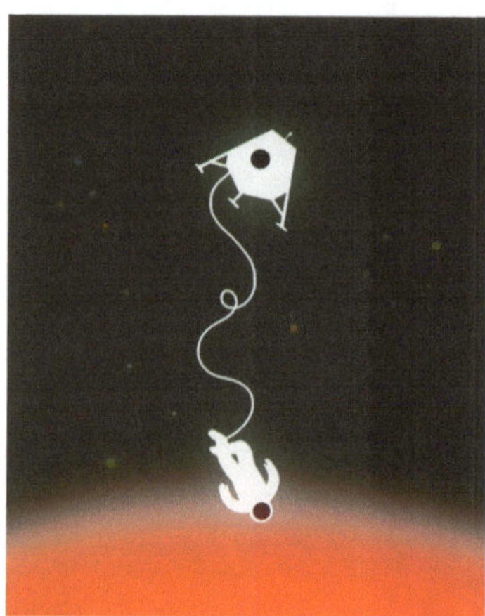

Escalade. Page 42

The Game. Page 56

THE ST

PUBLISHER'S LETTER

MEET THE STANDARD

In my experience, asserting a performative standard is a dangerous proposition. Just how dangerous it can be is explored in the final piece in this magazine—the only work of nonfiction in the issue.

As Lucky Ned Pepper says to Rooster Cogburn in Charles Portis's *True Grit*, my invitation for you to enter our unfamiliar arena is "bold talk for a one-eyed fat man." But to seek communal engagement requires leaving comfort and accepting resistance.

So what am I getting at?

This magazine exists because we believe there is a universal standard for art—specifically for fine fiction.

It is not controversial to claim that technology—artifacts writ large—can be measured against standards. No one confuses an iPhone with two Dixie cups connected by a string and calls them equivalent communication devices. An iPhone delivers a clearer, higher-fidelity signal.

Our proposition simply inverts that premise. Just as we can evaluate the fidelity of artifacts to technological standards, we can evaluate the fidelity of artifice—fiction and nonfiction—to psycho-technological standards. This inversion has not been well-received—until recently. The past decade of work by the writers and editors represented in this magazine, as well as the artists who have interpreted their work, suggests the tide is turning.

What ails our age is the assumption that the stories we're exposed to are silly distractions. The catastrophic result of this false dichotomy is the erosion of our individual, group, and collective capacities to make sense of our shared real world. Storytelling is not just "your opinion, man," nor is it reducible to the shifting verdicts of public opinion.

Story occupies a different domain entirely—what John Vervaeke calls *transjective* and what we recognize as mythic possibility. Story is the imaginal artifice we dream up; myth is the artifactual reality those stories become when they take hold. Myth does not mean fake, false, or escapist. It means the opposite. Myth is truer than true. It consists of recurring intelligible patterns that shape how we care for, act in, and come to understand reality.

History may not repeat, but it rhymes. Myth is that cyclical rhyme—empowering reason and enabling better, updated choices weighed against prior evidence.

William Butler Yeats expressed the profundity of this domain succinctly: "In dreams begin responsibilities." If we dismiss imaginal artifice as frivolous falsehoods, we suffer the consequences when those dreams realize as confusions.

This is what the standard of art concerns itself with—not perfection but coherence and responsible ownership of what our artifacts mean. There is no perfect story, and there never will be one. Just as there is no signal without noise, there is no meaningful story without imperfection. The goal is not flawless completion but consistent clarity.

So what, then, is the standard if not perfection?

It is ineffable. It cannot be reduced to a formula. I cannot do it. You cannot do it. Artificial intelligence systems cannot do it either. Like Justice Potter Stewart's observation in *Jacobellis v. Ohio*, we know it when we experience it. We seek it in order to be changed by it.

The stories in this magazine represent where we are now—not as an end point but as a commitment to continual improvement.

Which brings me to the final piece in this issue, "The Lives We Dream and Do Not Realize," the Story Grid mission statement. Inspired—perhaps haunted—by *Jerry Maguire*, it reflects the origin and reason behind our shared goal: to improve our translations of story artifice into artifactual myth with humility.

Spinoza put it even more plainly: *Veritas norma sui et falsi est.*

Truth is its own standard. We must reach for it together, knowing it will always remain beyond our grasp.

SHAWN COYNE / PUBLISHER

ILLUSTRATION BY VICTOR JUHASZ

THE TRUE STORY BENEATH THE BULLSHIT*

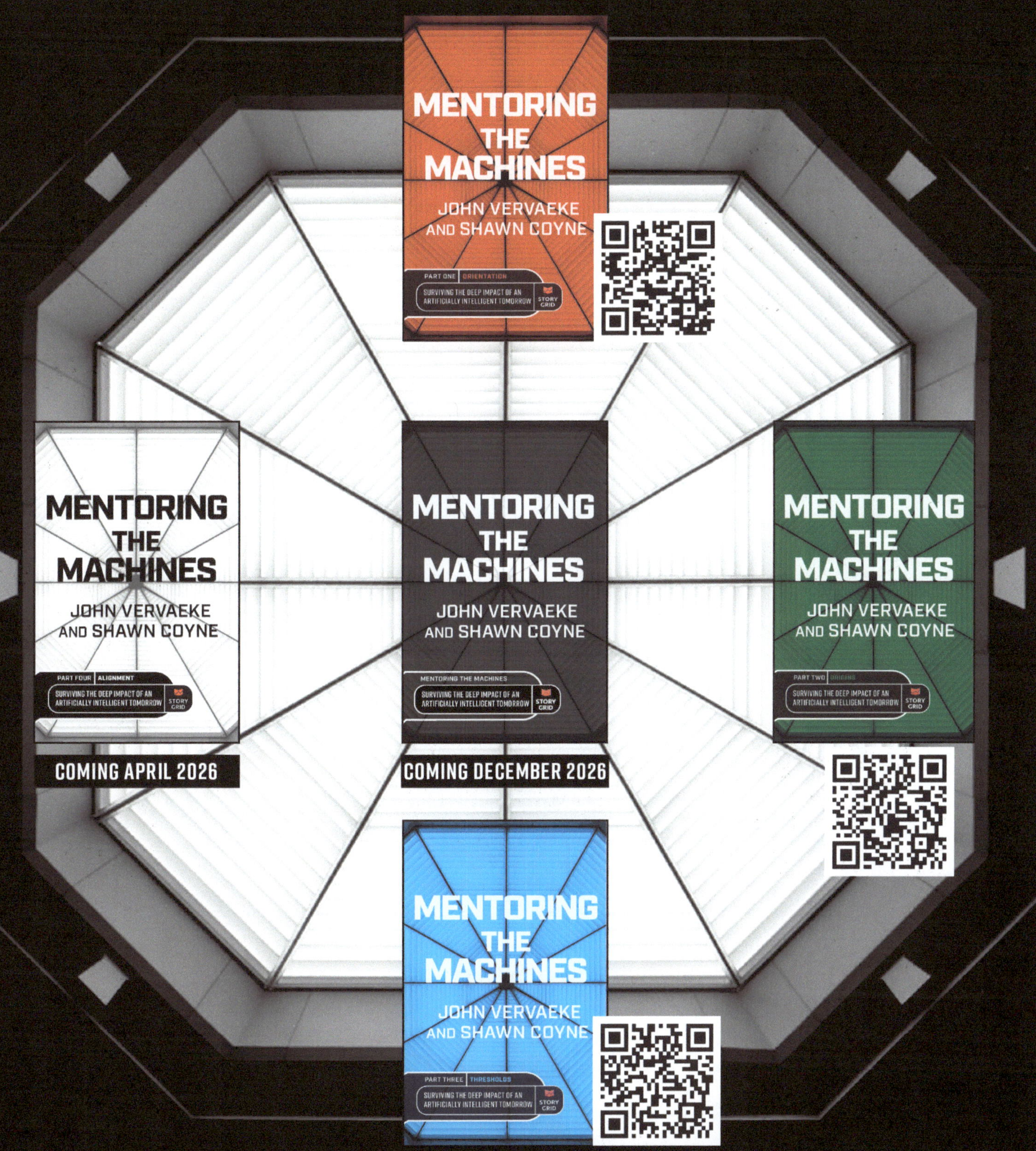

*"[The Bullshitter's] eye is not on the facts at all, as the eyes of the honest man and of the liar are, except insofar as they may be pertinent to his interest in getting away with what he says."
— Harry Frankfurt, *On Bullshit*

THE STANDARD is published by Story Grid Publishing, LLC
Nashville, Tennessee 37209
www.thestandard.pub
Each edition is available in book and eBook format
Ebook ISBN: 978-1-64501-111-8
Paperback ISBN: 978-1-64501-112-5
Printed in the USA

Tim Grahl: Editor in Chief,
Story Grid Chief Executive Officer,
Mentor

ILLUSTRATION BY VICTOR JUHASZ

SOCIAL STUDIES

BY **JEYLA BRIAR**
EDITED BY LAURA GRAVES

Ellen burst into the nearest stall, braced one hand against the toilet seat, and jammed the fingers of the other down her throat.

Her stomach fought, protested, threatened. To keep it all down. To turn it all into fat. Fat on her belly, fat on her thighs, fat on her face. She shoved harder, forcing her fingers further. Fuck, she'd jam her entire fist down her throat if that's what it took.

She gagged. Her mouth filled. A hot slurry of Hostess ejected into the toilet.

Ellen retched until the only thing left was long, black drools sliding off her chin. She flopped to the floor, drained and curling her upper lip at the puke-splattered crime scene. She ran a forearm across her face, smearing the mess off the best she could.

Hallway chatter briefly filled the bathroom followed by the sound of a door swooshing shut. Ellen leaned forward to flush the toilet. The lock behind her jiggled, and then the stall burst open.

"Uh-oh, did piggy eat too many Twinkies?" A cat-eyed girl, heavy-lidded under a pound of mascara, pointed her bejeweled iPhone at Ellen. Her lips twisted into a grin.

"Fuck off, Vera." Ellen scrambled to swipe the phone from her grip but whiffed, smacking the partition instead.

Vera backed up laughing, phone still aimed at Ellen.

A faucet kicked on outside the stall and Ellen's breath caught in her throat as she looked past Vera. Carly Allen leaned into the mirror, her reflection smoothing out a thick layer of ruby-red Dior Addict

ILLUSTRATION BY SASHA DAVYDOVA

across her lips. Straight black hair framed her porcelain skin and accented her emerald eyes. She smacked her lips together and sighed.

"Ellen, it smells like Little Debbie took a shit in here."

Vera snickered as Ellen shrank back against the toilet.

"Come on," Ellen pleaded. "We all do this."

Carly dropped the lip gloss into her Jacquemus micro and snapped it shut before turning to face Ellen. Vera stepped back and shifted the phone to Carly.

"The fucking exorcism you just performed into that poor toilet isn't something I've ever done." Her eyes cut to Vera. "How about you?"

Vera mouthed a pouty, exaggerated, "Nope."

Carly continued, "Purging is for little piggies who can't control themselves." Her eyes glazed past Ellen to the toilet, and she mouthed out a gag. "To be honest, I'm not sure I'll ever eat again after smelling that."

"I'm sorry." Ellen dug her nails into her fleshy arms. "I'm just so hungry all the time."

Carly's eyes rolled.

"That's fine. So tomorrow you sit with the fatties around the trough instead of with us."

Ellen stared at the floor. "I'll stop. I swear."

Carly cocked her head. "Can you stop? Can your giant piggy body control your giant piggy appetite?"

Vera oinked and then covered her mouth, giggling before swinging the phone back to Ellen to catch her response.

Ellen breathed deep, pulling the tears back from her eyes. "Yes."

"What do you think, Vera?" Carly asked. "Can she control it?"

Vera shook her head. "I don't think piggies like her can." She oinked again, louder this time.

"I'm not a pig," Ellen protested. "Can we please just forget this? I swear I won't do it again."

Carly frowned. "I think Ellen needs to admit she's a big ol' piggy." She positioned herself in front of the exit. Vera shifted behind her, raising the phone so it peeked over Carly's shoulder. "Right now."

Vera stepped forward. "A big ol' piggy loser."

Ellen's cheeks burned. A lonely sickness stirred in the pit of her stomach. She eyed Vera's phone. "Can you at least stop recording?"

"No, you need a reminder." Carly leaned in, pointing her polished finger at Ellen. "Now say you're a big ol' piggy."

Ellen held Carly's eyes, her jaw clinched shut.

Carly straightened and shrugged. "One less fatty following me around." She took a step back.

"Wait!" Ellen gasped, coming up to her knees.

Carly turned back and folded her arms.

The phone hovered. Voices floated in from the hallway.

Ellen's eyes dropped to the floor. "I'm a piggy."

Carly shook her head. "That's not what I said."

"I'm a big ol' piggy," Ellen mumbled.

"I can't hear you." Carly leaned in. "And this time, oink."

Ellen lifted her head. A tear broke free and trailed down her cheek. "I'm a big ol' piggy. Oink, oink, oink."

"Louder!" Carly slammed her palm into the stall, her eyes casting to a shade of black. "I want to hear you, piggy!"

"Oink like a real pig!" Vera blurted between laughs.

Ellen clamped her eyes, bit back a sob, and screamed, "I'm a big ol' piggy!" Her oinks, more sobs than pig snorts, echoed off the bathroom walls. Her chest ached. Her head throbbed.

Vera cackled. Carly nodded, a satisfied grin sliding across her face.

The bell rang.

In the hall, lockers slammed, and the door swung open, a stream of girls piling in. Vera tapped the screen with her thumb and slid the phone into the back pocket of her Agoldes.

Carly, her eyes green again, reached down and unrolled three sheets of single-ply toilet paper. She folded them, leaned over, and gently dabbed Ellen's face clean.

THE CANDYMAKER'S SON

BY **RYAN MCRAE**

EDITED BY TIM GRAHL

They killed my mother while I was busy serving breakfast. I hadn't seen her in seven years, since I was a young boy. But when I saw her swinging from the calibus tree and looked past the brokenness of her death, she was as I remembered—tall with long black hair pulled back in a tight bun. I felt like I was looking at a memory, a sketch of who she was.

Her death pulled at my sentimentality. But I reminded myself, she was a foolish woman, never selling anything at market with her useless crafts while my father risked his life on the sea trying to provide for our family. When the Balator military showed up on the island, saving us from a life of fish and trees, of poverty and weakness, I decided to join up and pull my own weight.

I had hoped to be something better, but she forbade me to go, trying to keep me for hers and hers alone. While she went off to help the babbling elderly of our town, I left, the only reminder of her my eyes, these bright green eyes. They shone like leaves under the sun just after a rain.

"Another forester hung," Ander said beside me, breaking me out of my trance. "She snuck into the camp last night. Boris and Gatter found her."

ILLUSTRATION BY SASHA DAVYDOVA

Ander was a forester, but his eyes were a muted green, like moss. I was envious that his eyes didn't betray him as quickly as mine did. He came from the far side of the island. He was a runner for the camp, delivering messages.

"What was she trying to do?" I asked.

He didn't know she was my mother. Ander couldn't keep a secret to save his life. If anyone knew that the woman trying to sneak into the camp was my mother, I'd probably be swinging beside her.

"Don't know. She just snuck in and was going from cabin to cabin. She made a run for it. The stable boy found her and turned her in. Now the lucky bastard is going to the capital." He paused and said, "Did you put in for a transfer again?"

I turned away from the tree and said, "Yeah, but they aren't going to take me." I pointed to my eyes. "You?"

He nodded. "I guess we just wait for our denial."

I wanted to become a chef for the emperor, and Ander hoped to be an engineer—worlds that had the potential to be ours if we could prove ourselves. Worlds we wanted to be a part of instead of this gods-forsaken island. Once all the trees were cut down, we'd go to the capital, but Ander and I would be old men by then. I'd be serving rabbit stew with gnarled hands. The capital was our path.

A scream rang through the camp.

We ran to the training yard and saw one of our foresters holding a sword, keeping two of the Balator soldiers at bay.

"That's Ebb—the stable boy. What in gods is he doing?" Ander asked.

I knew him. He grew up in a village next to mine. He wanted to be a wood-carver like his father.

"Just set the sword down," one of the soldiers said.

"Never," Ebb said with steel in his voice.

The Balator soldier swung his sword, but Ebb blocked it. The other rushed in but underestimated Ebb's skill. Ebb lunged forward, thrusting his sword through the soldier. He grinned with teeth and lips stained black as he pulled the sword out of him.

The other Balator soldier swung rapidly in succession, and Ebb blocked each one with a face full of rage. He kicked the soldier in the chest, knocking him to the ground. Ebb lifted up his sword, and I felt like he was looking at me when he screamed in the old forester tongue—something terrible.

Before he could plunge his sword down, a blur rushed behind him and sent a slash through the air, cutting off Ebb's head.

My mind detached, and I felt vomit rise to my throat.

A large Balator man dismounted from his horse in one smooth motion. "Can someone explain to me what is going on?" Commander Aiko yelled. He was a muscular build, like an ancient thunder tree with white hair like new snow—just like all of the capital-born Balator soldiers.

The soldier saluted and said, "The stable boy was attempting to desert."

A murmur of astonishment went through the crowd. Deserting was unheard of—a spit in the eye of those who rescued us.

"He drew on us. We had no choice but to put the filthy frog-eyed cretin down," the soldier continued.

Frog-eyed cretin. I'd heard worse.

Without warning, Aiko backhanded the soldier hard, causing him to stagger back like he'd been hit by lightning.

"You had a choice to be better swordsmen. But you chose to be bested by a…" He caught a word but chose differently. "Stable boy." He handed him the reins to his horse. "You're the new stable boy now. Go take care of my horse." The new stable boy did as he was told.

Aiko went over to Ebb and searched through his bag, dumping it out, and then he dug through his pockets to see if he was stealing any coin to get off the island another way.

He pulled out a black pouch made of folded paper. When I saw it, something in my chest lurched, but I pushed it down—way down.

Instead of carefully unfolding the package, he tore it open. Inside was a handful of small, black soft discs. He smelled them and took a bite. He spat it out immediately as if he'd tasted something unpleasant and bitter. I saw the small stain on his teeth and lips—black like Ebb's.

"Can anyone tell me what this is?" Commander Aiko asked addressing the crowd.

Murmurs went through, and I could see they were mostly foresters mumbling. They all knew but didn't want to say. But they were cowards. They didn't want to help and be honorable. They still thought like frog-eyes.

I raised my hand and said, "I do, sir."

Commander Aiko took three strides to get to me. "What is it, soldier?"

"It's jan-joh. It's forester candy. Old people eat it."

Commander Aiko looked me up and down. "How long have you been at this camp?"

"I joined when I was eleven, sir."

"Joined, yes," he said with an eyebrow raised. "You're the cook here."

"Yes, sir," I said, feeling proud that he recognized me.

"You're the one who cured the soldiers of food poisoning when they ate the wrong fish. Your name?"

"Yes, sir. Low Private Kio, sir," I said. I felt my chest puff out a bit more. They ate tabio fish, but the Balator chef cooked it too long. My father taught me that if you cook it wrong, it will make you terribly ill, and only ginger tea will cure you.

He turned to Ander and said, "Low Private Ander, what did that traitor yell right before I separated his head from his neck?"

Ander stammered, and before he could find the courage to say it, Commander Aiko struck him hard across the face. Ander staggered back like he'd been hit by a massive wave. I felt my chest burn in fear.

He turned to me. "What did he yell, Low Private Kio?"

I readied myself for his blow. "Death to the invaders, sir."

Commander Aiko glared, and I felt his hot breath on my face.

I felt a spark in me. "I know where that's made." Pointing to the jan-joh. "It's a village close to where the stable boy lived." I looked over, and his eyes went wide.

"It's a village called Endabo."

I hadn't spoken that name in a long time. It felt foreign and clumsy on my tongue.

Commander Aiko gave a tiny grin with the stain still there. "Well done. This poison has become a nuisance. Other camps have reported your people deserting and telling the tale of a woman who sets people free. She's been taken care of, but I need to make sure jan-joh can't find its way back to us." He stepped closer to us and said, "Go and find where this is made and burn everything connected to this woman to the ground. I never want to see this again." He handed me the torn package. "So you know what you are looking for."

Commander Aiko spoke again, but his tone was covered in frost. "If you can find this poison, I will approve both of your applications for the capital. Do you think you can handle this simple task?"

My eyes went wide. I could go to the capital, become a chef, and work with real ingredients from around the world instead of the smatterings of options here.

"Yes, Commander Aiko," we said in unison.

"Do not fail me in this," he said with steel in his voice.

We saluted, and he walked off.

"Why did you lie?" Ander mumbled, rubbing his welted face. "Death to the invaders? Are you trying to get killed?"

"I gave us a way off this island. Didn't I?"

Ander laughed. "You're right about that. I will find you in the dark, Itzaoki. Nonsense, anyway. What do you think it means?"

I didn't say anything. I didn't want to give my mother any company.

Ander and I spent our time riding talking about our plans when we arrived at the capital—the sights we'd see. I wanted to visit the White Spires, and he wanted to see how the capital used the river alongside it to power most of the city. Our dreams now had finer points to them, and they felt closer to the ground.

When we camped, Ander would practice his sword work and I would gather herbs, find wild vegetables growing, and catch rabbits. As I wandered the forest the first day, I found myself alone, and I couldn't remember the last time I had that. When I looked up, I would see my mother hanging there in the trees. Part of me wanted to climb up and cut her down, and part of me felt a surge of anger at her. Nothing was to be done. I hadn't climbed a tree in a long time, and she wasn't really there. I decided to spend less time alone.

Ander scoffed at the yet again meal of rabbit stew, but what else was there? However, once he tried it, he fell in love with it. I could make anything ordinary into something wonderful. At night while we tried to sleep, we didn't talk about the jan-joh, and he didn't bring up what the soldier yelled. I guess we were just enjoying our time together before we left for the capital, perhaps going our different ways.

After four days of riding on an empty supply cart, we came to Endabo, a small fishing village along the sea with tiny huts. The huts looked weather worn with holes in the roof, the thatching falling apart. The village was quiet—not the bustling place I remembered.

We drove into the center of the village, and I saw where my father used to sell his fish. People from other villages would come for his catches, ignoring the other fishermen who brought in the typical and ordinary.

ARTWORK BY TIMOTHY HSU

He would tell me that the key to being a fisherman was not to let the big fish escape once you had them on your hook. He told me the big fish would tell the other fish. And the fish would laugh at you. Then you would go for the other fish, the smaller ones, the weaker ones, the easy catch.

He'd then point at the other fishermen selling the common fish and say, "We aren't like them. We don't let anyone get away. Do we, Kio?"

And I'd shake my head vehemently.

Then he would spend the day in the tavern buying drinks for his friends. When I'd ask to join him, he'd pat me on the head and say, "Someday, little one."

Then my mother would pull me away, back to the house to help her make jan-joh while my father sang bawdy songs and made his friends laugh.

"The village is quiet," Ander said.

We passed the houses, and I expected at least someone to come out and greet us and offer to take our horses. No one came out.

I found my old home, a small hut. I tried the door, but it was locked.

"Why do you think this is it?" Ander said, a line of suspicion in his voice.

I paused and pointed to the roof. "It's well-maintained, unlike the others."

Ander seemed to accept that answer.

I needed to be better at this. I couldn't risk him knowing.

"We can just burn it down if that's the house and get back. We can be at the capital by next week," Ander said.

Something shook loose from me. "Ander, you aren't thinking! If we burn down the whole village, if we are wrong and we don't make sure that the jan-joh is gone…"

"Why are you acting like this? Just light it on fire, and we can say it's gone!"

I took him by the collar of his tunic. "We get one chance at this, Ander. One." I shoved my finger in his face. "We get off this island and start new lives. It's easier for you with your dim eyes, the ones that don't almost glow in the dark. But you aren't going to ruin this for me because you're in a hurry!"

I shoved him down. I felt like giving him a beating, but I didn't want to explain why he was coming back to camp with a face full of bruises. Ander got up and dusted himself off.

"Are you here for the market?" a voice asked.

We turned and saw an elderly woman standing there. Her hair was pepper gray with jade-like eyes—not as bright as mine but bright. She was wrapped in a multi-fold gray robe, a small wooden carving knife sheathed at her side.

"I think it's closed today. No one is there." She pointed toward the empty square. It appeared there hadn't been a market in a long time.

I said, "No. We are here to—"

"The market is only open on rest days. Is today a rest day?" she said.

Ander threw up his hands in frustration. "We are looking for jan-joh, old woman. Do you know where it is?" He talked to her like she was an insolent child.

She looked at him and squinted. "You are much too young for that. And Itza isn't here. She's gone, but she said she is coming back. I hope she is coming back soon."

Itza, my mother, wasn't coming back soon.

From here I could see the sea and wondered what my father thought after I joined up, if he wondered what became of me. I pushed that down as soon as I thought about it.

"And that's her house?" Ander pointed.

The woman nodded.

"That's enough proof. Isn't it? That the jan-joh is in there?" he said.

I shook my head, and Ander looked furious. He wanted to get to his dream as fast as he could.

The old woman looked out into the distance. "I hope she comes back soon. Some of us are drifting now. Drifting... drifting. We just need a taste."

Ander and I exchanged a look. I took out the package of jan-joh. "This? This is what she gave you?" Something came to the surface of my mind, my mother packing up the jan-joh. I would help her as my father braved the sea or gulped down a beer. There was more. I shoved it all down.

The old woman looked at the black jan-joh and almost recoiled. "No, no. Ours is blue. And green on Creation Day. That's for someone else."

"Maybe this Itza left some of the jan-joh in the house," I said.

Her eyes lit up a bit.

"Maybe we could go in and help find it?" I continued.

"Yes," she said, clapping her hands. "We just need a bit. Zarra just sings now. She's drifting far. If we drift for too long, it's hard to come back. We forget to eat. We forget to do other things besides sleep. We drift along. We just need a taste."

Ander looked at me with impatience. I held up a hand.

"Let us help you find it. Do you have a key for Itza's house?" I asked.

"Yes, but only if it's important." I found her staring at me more, looking like she misplaced something, and my face would tell her where to find it.

I grabbed her by the shoulders and shook her "It's important! We are trying to help you find the jan-joh, and then we will leave!" I said.

"I will get the key. Don't hurt me, Itzaoki," she cried.

I felt my heart split in two, hearing the name my mother called me when I would awake in the dark with nightmares as a child.

Ander's eyes went wide, and his face went red. "I will find you in the dark, Itzaoki."

He put his hand on his sword. "Itzaoki. Son of Itza." His eyes were lit with fury.

I placed my hands up. "If I had told Commander Aiko the truth, he would have run me through. But now we can be heroes, Ander. Let's just find the jan-joh, burn it all down, and head to the capital."

Ander took a step back. "He'll never send the son of a traitor." He drew his sword. "Or one who helped him." He lunged at me.

I jumped back and drew mine.

"Don't do this, Ander," I said, blocking his blows but just barely. "We can go."

He swung hard, and my arm quivered under the blow. He saw my weakness and kept his attack coming. I staggered back and lost my footing. I fell on my back, and my sword fell out of my hand, too far to reach.

Ander pinned me down and said, "The commander will be pleased. I will think of you when I reach the capital, Kio. But not for long."

He lifted up his sword, but before I could scream, his eyes suddenly went wide. He opened his mouth to say something, but blood poured out as he slumped over to one side. The old woman pulled the small carving knife out of his head and then wiped it on her robes as if she'd done it a hundred times.

"I'm glad you came back, Kio. You are Itza's son. I am…" She paused. "Rigana. My name is Rigana." She handed me the key to my mother's home and wandered back to her hut.

* * * * * * *

The hut was just as I had left it. The one room had a small stove and large wooden table with bowls and spoons on it along with her rolling pin. The small larder had various jars of sugars and spices. In the corner was my mother's bed, neatly made.

It didn't take me long to search the hut. There wasn't any jan-joh.

I was going to come back empty-handed, and Ander was dead. Maybe I could explain that away by saying he ate the jan-joh and ran, but I didn't believe the story no matter how many times I told it to myself. I felt my dreams of going to the capital break apart, and the pebble in my chest started to burn. My mother came looking for me and ruined everything I'd built up in the seven years since I'd joined the Balator.

I took the rolling pin and smashed it into the wooden table over and over. I felt my arms give out, so I sat on the floor and wept. Why did she have to go into the camp and ruin my life? What was she hoping to do? Turn me into a deserter?

I pushed away the questions that didn't serve me and made a decision. I'd just burn down the hut and tell Commander Aiko what happened. I'd most likely hang, but I'd die telling the truth with a chance of mercy.

I reached in my pocket for matches and found the package of black jan-joh instead.

I held a piece of it between my fingers and put it against my nose. I could already smell some of the herbs she used. It wasn't a danger to me now. I knew there was no hope outside of the army, and there were no soldiers for me to attack. But if I could recreate this and make it a weapon or useful tool for the Balator, I might find myself on the shore of the capital instead of the end of a rope.

I closed my eyes for a second and put the piece of jan-joh in my mouth. It was rich and sweet on my tongue. I touched my lip and drew back a black stain. I chewed and held it in my mouth, tasting every ingredient, making notes in my head.

I sat down at the table. I thought about getting a drink of water. My throat was suddenly parched and my head light. I was hot but equally cold. Before I could stand up, the world melted away.

* * * * * * *

The taste in my mouth is bitter, so bitter.

Then I smell the sea, the salt in the water.

I am on the shore. I can still hear the Balator in the village. My younger self is standing with my mother and clutching his belongings. He is crying hysterically. My father is standing in front of his boat. I can see the not small sack of coins along with enough food to last him weeks. The coins have the Balator insignia on them.

"You have to take him, or they will, Kathuo!" my mother screams at my father.

"I won't," he says.

She shoves me toward him. "Please! He will not survive! They will come for him. And you brought them here. You went out too far, past the boundary, and they found us."

He points at my younger self with rage. "You think this boy can survive out there? With those eyes you cursed him with?"

I forgot how dark my father's eyes were.

He shoves my younger self down and strikes my mother hard across the face. She staggers back but returns with a face of steel.

"I hope they find you, Kathuo. I hope everyone sees your eyes and calls you coward and betrayer." She spits in his face.

I hear a storm coming. My mouth burns.

I see my mother hold on to me as the soldiers come. They pry her from me. I cry for her—and a soldier says the crying is over. I am a man now. I have joined the Balator army. I'm placed in a wagon along with the other children. One child tries to wake herself up as if this was a dream, but the wagon rolls on and on, farther and farther away. My mother chases the wagon as long as she can. Everything fades except her cry:

Itzaoki! Abakai-tao! Abakai-tao!

Kio. Son of Itza! I will find you in the dark!

I see her alone making jan-joh, but this time it is black like a funeral flower. It is filled with all that the Balator took from us. And she takes out a small blade and slices the jan-joh with precision.

I suddenly came to and felt the hot tears on my face. I felt my life unraveling, the lies unspooling. I lost count of them from my father to the Balator. My mother was what I was hunting for. She was what imbued the jan-joh. She kept the elderly from drifting and helped them remember. She was gone now, hung from a tree trying to find me, wanting me to remember the truth of it all. The grief took me like a riptide, out far into the sea of it.

After a while, after tears ran out, I went to the wooden sink and washed my face. I looked in the small mirror and saw my eyes. How they glowed. I felt the pebble in my chest burn white hot. I would go to the capital. I would go and burn it to the ground.

I went to the pantry, got out the ingredients, and started measuring.

It's said that the Balator hung the Silver Mother from a tree. Her children with silver smiles crept into the camps and placed the sacred jan-joh in the hands of others, waking them up, helping them remember the sounds of the sea and the shade of the trees. They hung the Balator from every tree branch they could, poisoning their food with the forbidden herbs of the forest, and took their ships for their own. And the Silver Son, the Itzaoki, is said to still wander the forest, making his jan-joh of every color. For that we are grateful.

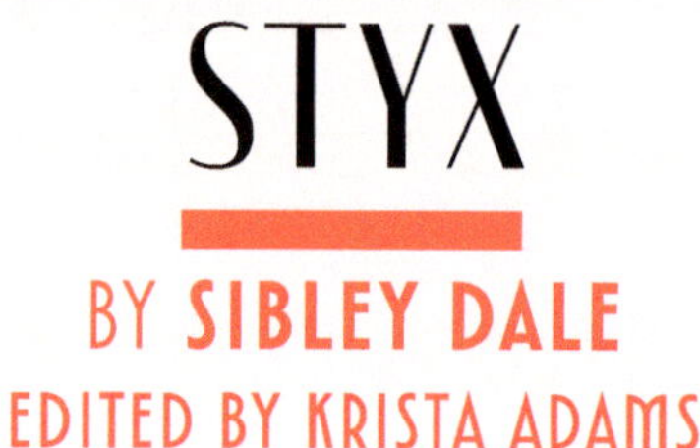

STYX

BY **SIBLEY DALE**
EDITED BY KRISTA ADAMS

You rip your arm free. His nails rake your skin. Blood throbs back into your fingers. You clutch torn fabric to your chest. Cold air bites the skin beneath.

The water hits your thighs—cold, thick, dragging at your legs. Your foot plunges into soft muck. The stench rises: rot, sulfur, something dead.

Behind you, the hounds erupt. Chain link rattles and sings. Your gut clenches.

Branches scrape your arms. Wet moss slaps your face. His laughter follows—unhurried, pleased. It echoes off the water and finds you.

You run. Your breath shreds. Your legs burn. You keep running.

Your back slams bark. You slide down, chest heaving. The air is sulfur and rot, so thick it coats your tongue, your throat, your lungs.

Heat crawls over your skin. Something moves on your neck. Legs. You slap it away. Your hand comes back black with swamp muck.

Sweat trickles down your face, between your breasts. It finds every cut and lights it up—a constellation of small fires on your arms, your legs.

The taste in your mouth is death, wet decay on your tongue. You smell like the swamp now. Like the swamp and fresh blood.

Your own meat stink chokes you.

ARTWORK BY **VENTIKO**

The dogs bay. Louder. The sound presses against your ribs.

A growl tears from your throat. You snap off a dead branch. The wood bites your palm. You grip it like a spear, push off the trunk. The water swallows you again, cold shock climbing past your waist.

You lunge back to the edge, regaining purchase. Your feet search for roots, for anything solid. You hug the trunks. Something swarms your ankle—tiny fire, everywhere at once. You lurch sideways, slapping. Ants.

A hiss stops you cold. A snake coils back, head level with your hand. Another slides past your thigh into the water. Your whole body shudders.

Moonlight scatters through the canopy. You can't trust what you see.

Your foot finds what looks like ground. It isn't. You plunge to your hip, water flooding your mouth. You spit, gag, drag yourself up.

Moss tangles your face. You claw it away. Thorns rake your forearm. You rip free, leaving skin behind.

You stab at every dark shape. The stick hits nothing. Hits water. Hits wood.

Yips. Snarls. The crack and crash of bodies through brush. Closer. They don't hesitate. They know where you are.

Your legs turn to stone. Each step costs more than the last.

Branches hook your shirt, your hair. They drag you back. You wrench forward, fabric ripping. Your lungs won't fill. Each breath is half what you need.

The mud takes one shoe. You keep moving. It takes the other. Now your bare feet find every root, every sharp thing hidden below.

The water finds your cuts. It burns—salt and rot seeping in.

The stick shakes in your fist. You can't make it stop.

Every step drives something new into your feet. Thorns. Splinters. You can't stop. You leave blood in the water behind you.

The dogs' pitch changes. Higher. Hungrier. Birds explode from the trees—a roar of wings. Your heart seizes.

You look back. Your foot finds nothing. You pitch forward. Water closes over your face—cold, total, black.

You sink. The cold swallows you whole. Green darkness closes over your eyes.

You claw upward. Your feet hit muck. You shove off. Something punches through your foot—in through the sole, out through the top. The pain whites out everything.

Your face breaks the surface. You gasp, choke—swamp water floods your mouth, slick and rotting.

Your hands rake water, weeds, nothing solid. You can't move. The wood through your foot holds you like a nail.

You arch, twist—something slides past your calf. Scales. Muscle. Your stomach heaves. Bile burns your throat. You try to scream. You choke on it instead.

The dogs crash through. Moonlight catches their teeth. Their eyes find you.

Drool swings from their jaws. Their smell hits you—wet fur, hunger, something older than fear.

The stick slips from your fingers. Your body goes quiet.

Your hands find the broken branches beneath you. You grip them. You pull yourself down.

You breathe in—one long, full breath. Then you let go.

The water closes over you. The howling warps, softens, fades.

THE RESIDENT GHOST

BY **BRENT G. SPALDING**

EDITED BY TIM GRAHL

The whole thing starts with me following a ghost. Not a literal ghost—the idea is absurd to me—but a man I spot purchasing a whipped mocha latte, Pete's favorite, from a curbside coffee stand. He wears the same white jeans and gray and white sweater that Pete often sports, but what clinches my attention is the black face mask over his nose and mouth. Pete always wears one in public, even prior to the pandemic, cautious that his heart, enlarged from a birth defect, can't handle illnesses most of us take for granted. That very defect took his life this morning, just minutes after I went to the cafeteria to get breakfast for his sister, Lisa, after several nights of sitting vigil with her at his bedside.

The crowds, thick for a rainy Thursday night, keep me from getting a clear look, but a certainty grows in me, hot and fierce, that I have to reach this man as he walks up Main. My lower back hurts, but I tighten the straps of my backpack and quicken my pace. I follow him for almost a mile, past the cafés and bars, until I'm jogging a hundred feet behind him. Rain pelts my head with ice-cold pellets, soaking my hair and running down my face in rivulets. My rational mind scolds me, but my obsession to see this man up close overwhelms it.

When I catch up with him, the man clearly is not Pete. He is too tall, the sweater actually yellow and blue and a different pattern, his jeans a light gray. He stands in line to board a city bus and tosses his finished mocha latte to the sidewalk before boarding. As rain stings my eyes, I watch him through the windows until he takes a seat.

The rain stops as the bus rolls away. I pick up the discarded drink container and toss it into the woven metal trash container by the bus stop bench, grief aching in my chest.

Mist rolls up from the river, thickening as it creeps across the street. The streetlights flicker and the stoplights flash with red. I catch the name of the four-floor condominiums looming overhead. Cliffport Estates. *Shit.*

I'm standing in front of the home of my ex-boyfriend, Tyler Baines. I recognize the facade, having bookmarked it on Google Earth soon after he dumped me for the wealthy Steven Belmonte three years ago.

A question nags at me. Did I follow "Pete" to Tyler's doorstep on purpose from a subconscious desire to reconnect? When I left the hospital, I couldn't bring myself to return to the one-bedroom bungalow I share with Pete. I didn't even go back to get my phone charger or a change of clothes.

"An astounding novel of J.R.R. Tolkien proportions"
— Steven Pressfield, Bestselling author of *Gates of Fire* and *The War of Art*
THE SAND SEA
MICHAEL McCLELLAN
MICHAEL McCLELLAN
ABSOLUTE ADVENTURE

I needed to be around people, or so I told myself, and spent the day wandering downtown near the Riverside District, and Cliffport Estates, with only my backpack and $31.49 in cash. The patrons of the bistros and cafés kept me company, creating an illusion of normalcy to distract me from the calamity that had become my life. Now, I find myself at Tyler's doorstep.

Without thinking, I glance at the second-floor balcony of the unit I know he shares with Steven. Someone stands on the balcony, a face illuminated in the glow of a cell phone. Tyler? A flash of panic flows through me. I can't let him see me in this state, grieving and chasing ghosts.

My heart leaps as I turn to go and glance across the street. A man like the one I was following stands under a street lamp on the sidewalk along the river bank. But this man's sweater really is gray and white in the familiar pattern I know so well. As he looks at me, he lifts his face mask to sip from a coffee container, allowing me a brief glimpse of his lower face before lowering the mask back down.

"Pete." The name croaks out of my throat, frozen from the cold and damp. Mist shrouds him as he lifts his hand with the coffee cup, as if to send me cheers. Or farewell. An icy chill shivers down my spine, weakening my legs. Fearing I'll lose him in the fog, I step into the street to cross over.

Light blinds me. The screaming bellow of a horn blasts and tires screech as a truck barrels from the mist straight at me.

Pain crushes through my shoulders as something pulls me backward from my backpack's straps. The truck rattles past, the horn still blaring as it fades into the fog. I fall backward into cold, muddy water, the

backpack cushioning my impact on the flooded lawn of Cliffport Estates. I spit out the taste of dirt and grass.

Someone in a red shirt lies next to me in the mud. He sits up and kneels at my side. I try to sit up, but I am stuck on my back from the weight of the pack, squirming like a bug on a pin.

Then, a familiar voice emerges from a shadowed face framed with damp, blond hair. "Kurt?"

He reaches a hand down to me, and I grasp it. The streetlight catches his face, and I can see clearly it is

ILLUSTRATION BY CLARE KIM

Tyler. In my stupor of shock over the near collision, I don't feel any actual surprise.

"Kurt," he says, taking my pack and looking me over with a smile. "I *thought* it was you coming up the street, but I couldn't believe it! I came down to see just as you… Well, thank God I was here."

A pain radiates from my hip down my right leg as I stumble forward. Tyler places a hand on my shoulder. "Are you okay?"

I start to shake my head, but the pain dissipates as I take a step. "Yes, just a cramp, but I'm fine."

He takes his hand off my shoulder and motions with his head. "Follow me."

He keeps my pack as I follow him inside to the second floor. We enter his unit through a door across from the elevator, stepping into a white marbled foyer next to a kitchen.

"Well, this is ruined," Tyler says, picking at his shirt, which is probably silk. He has come a long way since our days of thrift store wardrobes. He strips it off and throws it into the kitchen sink. "What the hell were you doing out there?"

I stare at him, unable to formulate an answer that would make sense.

"Oh, forget it," he says, waving his hand as he places my backpack near on the tile. "We can talk later. Right now, we need to clean up." He strips off his jeans and drops them to the tile floor before walking naked to a bathroom on the right. His body hasn't changed in the years since I last saw him, still trim and muscular. I involuntarily suck in my gut. He comes back wearing a white bathrobe and holding another in his hand. "I can't give this to you covered in all that mud. Take off your clothes."

I remove my jacket and shirt, dropping each to the tile, and then slide off my shoes and soaked socks. My hands hesitate as I unbuckle my belt. I look up at Tyler. "Some privacy, please?"

"Oh, for chrissake," Tyler says. "It isn't like you can show me anything I haven't seen before." He lets out an exaggerated sigh of exasperation. "Oh, alright, I'll avert my gaze."

He turns around and I remove my jeans and underwear before stepping behind him and into the bathroom. He hands me the white bathrobe with one hand, the other covering his eyes.

"Use the shower," he says. Slightly parting his fingers, he adds with a sly smile, "You filthy thing."

Tyler has a tendency to "queen-it-up" (his term) when he is nervous, an exaggerated femininity of gesture and voice. It helps me feel better. He's as baffled as I am by our sudden circumstances.

I shut the door, twist the lock, and then hang the bathrobe from a hook.

The shower feels glorious. I let the warm water flow over me, lathering up a body gel from a dispenser built into the shower wall. I haven't showered since Pete went into the hospital, and days' worth of dirt flow off me as the warm water eases the aches in my muscles. The doctors intubated Pete at the hospital three days ago so he could breathe past the fluid in his lungs. Fluid, meaning blood from a leaking heart valve. Then, sixteen hours ago, his organs began shutting down.

I press another button on the shower wall to dispense shampoo and rub it through my gritty hair. As I rinse in the warmth, I feel the gold chain around my neck. My fingers play along the jagged edge of the pendant, a gift from Pete that I haven't taken off since he gave it to me. I lean my head against the shower tile and let the warm water run down my face. I wasn't even with him when it mattered most, holding his hand as he drew his last breath. And what would he think of me showering at Tyler's home just hours later?

I twist the lever to stop the water and towel off, steam swirling in tendrils through the bathroom air as I step onto a fluffy white bathmat. I put on the bathrobe and swipe the mirror with its puffy sleeve. My face is drawn and pale with dark lines under my eyes from lack of sleep. No wonder I was stalking strangers and hallucinating a phantom Pete.

I hear a trickling sound behind me, and a shadow moves behind the misted glass door of the shower. I wrap the robe tighter as a chill breeze brushes past me. *Someone is in the shower.* Had Tyler come in while I was distracted by my reflection in the mirror? I think of the man I saw across the road and shiver.

I jolt when I hear a banging at the door. "You still alive in there?" Tyler.

"I'm done," I say. The shadow is gone, and the room returns to its humid warmth. I look back at myself in the mirror, noticing for the first time the robe has red scripted letters on the right breast spelling *Tyler.*

Tyler opens the bathroom door and steps in. He looks at me and frowns. "You still look like hell."

"Thanks," I say, glancing at the shower for evidence of the shadow. All I see is the fogged glass and movement of dissipating steam.

Tyler reaches down and fingers the pendant around my neck. I flinch as he squints his eyes, looking at the inscription.

"What's this say… '*Watch me and thee we are absent another.*' What does that mean?"

"It's part of a Bible quote." I can't bring myself to mention Pete has the other half. Or had. It vanished amid the chaos of doctors and nurses rushing him from the ER to intensive care.

Tyler cringes and releases the pendant before flicking off the bathroom light. He walks over to another door and swings it open. "You can sleep in here tonight."

A shaft of light spills into the darkness. Paintings line the walls, and two canvases on separate easels sit in the middle of the floor, each with subjects I can't make out in the dark. The paint smells faint, like it dried long ago. At the far end of the room is a metal-framed day bed.

"Your studio?" I step inside, but Tyler yanks me back by the shoulder and slams the door shut. I glare at him, but he turns toward the living room.

"I made you something to eat." His eyes glint as he motions toward a glass coffee table with two filled wineglasses and a plate with a sandwich.

I follow him to the table where the wine glistens dark red in the flickering glow of a gas fireplace. A white wall clock with chrome Roman numerals reads nine thirty-one. The air feels still, not warm and not cool, and translucent white curtains filter the city lights coming from the bay windows facing the river. I peek out and see only darkness, thick fog moving past in deep gray tendrils.

Tyler sits down on the sofa. "Sit," he says, motioning to a matching chair across from him. He points toward the sandwich as I sit down, his piercing green eyes following me. "Your favorite, I recall. Tuna salad on rye."

I sit down and stare at the sandwich.

"Your clothes are in the washer," he says. "Eat."

He watches me until I pick up the sandwich. My mouth waters at the aroma, but I think of the twenty pounds I gained since I last saw Tyler, and again I'm comparing myself with his still-perfect physique. My stomach tightens with nausea, ashamed to be thinking like this under my circumstances.

I force a smile. "This looks great, but I'm not very hungry."

"Just take a bite," he says. "Then we can dish about what brings you to my decadent part of town."

I nibble at the corner of the sandwich. My stomach growls at the flavor, and the nausea gives way to a ravenous hunger. I finish the sandwich quickly, washing it down with the wine.

Tyler smirks. "Not hungry, huh?"

"Guess I was," I say and then point to the embroidered name "Steven" on his bathrobe. "So, is he around?" I consider how awkward it would be if Steven came in the front door to see the two of us in their robes drinking wine.

"He's not here." Tyler picks up the wine bottle and refills my glass. "How about you? What brings you here on this ghastly night? Trouble in paradise?"

He met Pete once, just after we moved in together, when he and Steven ran into us at a gallery exhibit a few years back. Tyler referred to us as Batman and Robin because we wore face masks months after the pandemic mandates had expired. Pete laughed politely at that, but on the bus ride home wondered aloud what a classy (and hot, he observed, for a man pushing forty) man like Steven Belmonte saw in that "bitch diva" Tyler.

"It's a long story." My fingers twitch as I drink more wine. "You sell any of your work?"

Tyler's shoulders stiffen at the question. "I'm mostly just keeping in practice, trying to hone my skills. You?"

"I haven't had anything worth selling yet either, but I keep up the practice." My voice drops off, my mind shifting to the sketches I made of Pete intubated in the hospital.

Tyler leans forward. "Hey, why don't you sketch me? Let me see how you've improved."

I fidget my bare feet against the soft rug. "Let me see some of your recent work first."

A thin smile forms on Tyler's face. "There will be time for that later."

He stands up and opens a cabinet by the fireplace. He pulls out a new sketching pad and container with pencils, placing them in my lap. Panic rises in my chest. What if he wants me to do a nude, like the first time we…

"More wine, please," I say.

Tyler sighs and hands me the bottle. I pour what is left of it, hoping in the delay he will forget his request. I sip while Tyler stands up and walks across the room. My eyes follow him as he opens the door to his studio and steps inside. I feel myself relax. My head swims gently as wine flows down my throat. The day's events begin to feel distant, almost like a dream.

Tyler emerges from the studio, closing the door with a sharp click. "Okay," he says, "you've had more wine. Now, earn your room and board and sketch me." He stands before me and pulls off his bathrobe before reclining on the sofa. "Just like when we took Art 101—The Human Nude."

There is no avoiding it. As when I saw him strip earlier, I'm struck by how beautiful he still looks, his body a golden tan and perfectly sculpted. My face grows warm as I fumble with the pencils on the coffee table.

"That was at least Art 201," I say and almost add, *And our model wasn't even half as easy on the eyes*, but refrain. I pick a pencil that looks best for the job and then flip open a blank page.

I feel my shoulders relax at the familiarity of holding a pencil. My head swims a bit from the wine as I swipe the pencil tip on the paper. Tyler holds his pose, his eyes intent upon me. I sketch in silence, the lines and shadows forming on the page bringing me a gentle peace over the agonies of the past few days. I feel I have a purpose again.

Tyler starts humming. I ignore it at first and then realize he is humming "My Heart Will Go On." I start to laugh but then stop sketching and glare at him. "Oh, you *stop* that!" I say it with a lighthearted flourish, the word "stop" coming out as "st-*hop*."

Then he shouts, "Rose! *Jack!* Rose! *Jack!*" in alternating baritone and falsetto.

I crumple the napkin my sandwich had been on and throw it at him.

"Now, *there's* my little Kurt!" Tyler's face beams.

I wave him off, examining my almost finished sketch and note that Tyler's serious expression looks pretentious. I consider altering it, maybe giving him a bit of a Mona Lisa smirk, but decide against it. I sign and date the drawing. "Here." I hold out the sketching pad to him.

Tyler stretches out his arm and takes it. He looks at the sketch, his eyes narrowing as he nods. "This is good. It really captures my attributes."

I wonder if he's being sarcastic. "Thanks, but it isn't as good as I can do."

Tyler shrugs and sets the pad down on the coffee table open to the sketch. "I'll go check on your clothes." He shimmies his shoulders as he puts the robe back over them. As he tightens the cloth belt, I notice that the embroidered name on the chest isn't "Steven," but "*Steven's*."

I look at the red embroidery on the robe I am wearing. Sure enough, "*Tyler's*." They wear each other's name. I chuckle at its possessiveness. I'm sure it was Tyler's idea.

As Tyler disappears into a small hallway, I stand up, my head swimming from the wine. I feel the weight of the pendant against my chest, and an image of Pete at the hospital flickers in my mind, the nurses unhooking his still form from the machines that had failed to keep him alive.

What am I doing here? Guilt weighs on my shoulders as I realize Tyler is the first person I have sketched since Pete at the hospital. An overwhelming need to see those last sketches flows through me, and I look toward the kitchen for my backpack. It leans against a metal garbage can on the tile, a pool of water underneath.

I gasp, stumbling over to it and grabbing the top handle. Horror sparks through me as I hear a thick sloshing. I unzip the main compartment. The sketch pad is soaked in muddied water, my set of pencils soiled in the muck. I pull out the pad, trying to open the pages, but they are stuck together and start falling apart. Water flows from the paper, staining my hands with gray rivulets of bleeding graphite. I groan, the pad sloshing as I drop it back into the pack. A reflective smiley face Pete had sewn onto the blue fabric gleams in the light, mocking my discovery.

I struggle to breathe. All of Pete's last hours, lost. My head throbs as I struggle to keep my composure. I'm not ready to talk to Tyler about this. I can't bear his sympathies over my catastrophic life next to his flight in the high life.

My hands shake, and tears blur my vision when a sound in the kitchen kills the escaping grief. I look up, but it isn't Tyler in the kitchen. A shadow, like the one in the bathroom, stands near the dark kitchen over a small bar. I hear glass clinking with ice and the slosh of liquid pouring. The figure is featureless and dark, a three-dimensional shadow with movements from its arms like they are shaking or stirring something. Just like Pete would, while mixing us Friday night martinis.

I try to stand up, crying out as a sharp pain cascades up my right leg to my hip. I sit back down, the pain abating, but the muscles in my chest and arms begin twitching, a sensation like hands grabbing my body and pushing me down to the floor. I try rolling over, my thrashing arms meeting nothing but air.

Then it is gone. I sit up, glancing through the kitchen. The space in front of the small bar is empty, a single bulb flickering above it. I tighten the robe around my body, shaking my head to clear my thoughts as my head swims. The wine on a near-empty stomach is affecting me. The shadow, the touches, just illusions from a mind drowning in grief, the pain in my leg, a muscle cramp from the hard landing outside when I almost got hit by a truck.

I decide it's time to leave. I head into the small hallway to find Tyler. It is dark and I can't find a switch for light. The wall curves to the right, so I turn in that direction.

The smells hit me first. Cigarette smoke, sweat, and alcohol. My head swims as a vibration buzzes the air, a throbbing that shakes the floor at my feet and the bones in my chest. Shadows move around me,

dark against dark. But instead of panic, I feel relaxed, a familiarity of the scene calming me. It is like a night at the clubs, Tyler and me dancing together and with strangers under the deafening, throbbing beats of music.

The cool metal of the pendant weighs against my chest, and I reach for it, holding it in my hand and tracing the smooth zigzag of the dividing edge against my thumb. A flush of shame falls upon me, like I'm cheating on Pete.

A flash of light bursts around me and the sensations stop. I stand near a washer and dryer that softly hums as clothes tumble inside. A painting of shirtless dancing men hangs on the wall. I recognize it as The Crush Tavern, where Tyler and I spent countless nights.

"Hey."

I jump and turn around. Tyler stands with his hand on the light switch, leaning against the doorjamb. In the other hand, he holds a fresh glass of dark wine.

I can still smell it on me. The smoke. The sweat. Confused by a mingling desire and repulsion, I turn to the dryer, looking for the switch to shut it off. "I want my clothes."

Tyler sets his glass down on a small table and pulls me back.

My head aches as I try to keep tears from bubbling up. I can't bring myself to tell him what just happened. "I want to go home."

"Don't leave."

"What about Steven? He might not appreciate the two of us together in nothing but your monogrammed bathrobes."

"Kurt, listen to me." Tyler's eyes narrow. "Steven is...gone. Like, forever."

My mouth drops open, but I can't find any words to say.

"About a year ago," Tyler says, toying with the tie on his robe. "He...well, it was quick and unexpected, an accident..." Then he takes in a deep breath as tears glint in his eyes. "But he's still around, you know. Like he's stuck here." He picks up his wineglass and drinks half the contents.

"You're saying he's a *ghost*?" A shiver runs through me. *That shadow.*

He looks up for a moment, his eyes on the painting. Then he looks me in the eye and nods. "My very own resident ghost. I've read that love ending in such tragedy can do that. A spirit bound to a living beloved."

The image of Pete an hour ago flashes in my mind, standing on the other side of the road, embraced by mist.

A wave of shame and grief rolls through me. What am I doing here? What am I thinking? I rip open the dryer door, the clothes spilling out. I grab my jeans and shirt and pull off the robe.

Tyler pulls at the clothes. "Hey, Kurt, stop."

I yank myself backward, holding the wet clothes close to me. "I shouldn't be here," I say, walking down the hall. I turn a corner and then another. I expect to enter the main living area, but the hall continues on past two more corners. Confused, I stop and shake my head. I turn to go back the way I came and go around the corner, only to find myself facing a white wall, my previous path gone.

"Tyler!" My voice echoes, the light flickering.

"What the fuck? Tyler!"

The hall grows dark, and I push my back against the wall, grasping the damp bundle of clothes to my shivering body. A dim, bluish light pulses at the other end, around the corner I had just come. I edge along the wall, heading toward the light and calling Tyler's name.

As I turn the corner, a vibration again pulses through the walls, pounding through my chest. A paneled white door opens slightly ahead of me, the light and bass synth beat radiating from the other side. The door swings open as I approach.

I find myself at the threshold of Tyler's studio. I step inside, engulfed with the skunky sweet odor of reefer and cigarette smoke, sweat and alcohol, and the pinching, acrid odor of poppers. A half dozen easels stand in the room, figures on each canvas swaying and writhing to the beat.

A glow like red embers blazes around me and the room grows warm.

Behind me, Tyler's voice whispers like black velvet, "Stay."

I turn. He stands naked, a golden statue of chiseled flesh. Tyler gently tugs at my bundled clothes, and I let them go. He tosses them aside, and they vanish into the shadows. He takes my hands and pulls me toward him.

"It will be like it was," he whispers.

My body has changed, once again lean with the muscular chest and defined abs from years ago. I feel light and giddy as around me the paintings glow, displaying images from our days together as starving artists, our cement block studio with a large metal door that opens to the lower downtown streets.

I am back there, those streets of grease and broken glass, the acrid stench of overflowing garbage cans and skeletal remains of cars on streets that become seasonally dotted with the bursting colors of tents for the homeless, like forgotten flowers growing in the cracks of an alley. Images of ourselves nude and asleep on a bare mattress on a stained concrete floor, amid the aromas of paint, oils, acrylic, paper and glue, our canvases, bursting with colors, lining the walls with sensual landscapes. Our future together still lay ahead. We are going to make it. We are going to *be something.* I realize then I am smiling at the memory, smiling for the first time since Pete went under intubation three days ago.

A hand reaches from a canvas, dripping with oil and acrylic, and grasps my arm. A young man emerges, his naked muscles glistening with sweat and his eyes flashing in the ruby light. More figures emerge from the paintings, the room coming alive with blaring with music and glimmering lights, eager bodies coaxing me to dance.

"It can be like this forever," Tyler says, his fingers running down my neck to pull at the chain of my necklace.

The pendant dances against my chest, bringing a familiar aroma of coffee and chocolate. A soft hug and warm eyes. *Pete.*

Images flood my mind. *Pete yawning with a smile next to me. Pete making us dinner. Pete watching me paint. Pete holding my hand in a dark movie theater. His gentle kiss on my neck. His hand caressing my cheek.* Images of cozy domesticity, of trust and comfort. Of home. A fresh wave of yearning overwhelms me.

I pull back and shake my head. “No, Tyler.”

Hands from the men around us run down my back and chest, fingers reaching for my chain. Tyler steps forward, his hand on my chin, lifting my head to look into the luster of his green eyes. “But it was the best times of our lives, little Kurt. We should never have given it up, and now we’re both grieving in widowhood. Why not let all that go and let it be like before?”

I pull my arms away, shaking my head. “Wait… What?” I never told him about Pete.

Tyler straightens his posture and looks down at me. “Hell, Kurt, you reek of the grief. I smelled it a mile away.” His voice softens as his lips part, ready to kiss me. The figures dancing around us gather closer, pushing him toward me. “It opened doors and brought you back to me,” he whispers, his fingers caressing my pendant. “Just let go and it will be like it was.”

I clasp my hand around the pendant, its metal warm against my palm. “Get away!” I jerk my body around, twisting out of the groping hands and away from Tyler.

The room crackles and brightens, falling to silence. I stand alone with Tyler, the walls and easels with paintings of silent oil and acrylic, depicting the dancing men and scenes that a moment ago immersed us. Lights flicker red and blue from the windows facing the river. The air cools and flows into gentle motion.

Tyler grabs my wrist, his face red with anger. “Look what you did! It was almost done!”

I pull away and turn, but Tyler grabs me by the shoulders and steers me back to him. Except Tyler isn’t there any longer. Pete stands in his place, reaching his arms to embrace me.

“I can be him if you want,” he says, but the voice is still Tyler’s. “Or anyone you want. Just stay.”

I shut my eyes, unable to look at Pete with that voice, when a realization hits me like a brick. “You… you were who I saw across the street?”

When I open my eyes, Tyler has returned to his own form. “Kurt, I know you always loved me more than him. Why else come to me on the night he died?”

I push away from him with a grunt and leave the studio, heading toward the sound of the clock ticking in the living room. The clock reads nine forty-nine, barely twenty minutes from when I arrived, yet I had to have been here for over an hour.

I turn to the foyer, but Tyler steps in front of me, his voice bellowing, “You can’t leave, Kurt. It’s too late!”

Something in the living room flashes by me. The shadow. It moves toward the bay windows and glass door to the balcony. Blue and red lights flash against the white translucent curtains, punctuated by the brief whoop of a siren. The shadow passes through to the outside.

Tyler laughs, a choked, guttural sound. “Go ahead. Follow it. See for yourself. You can’t go back.”

I open the sliding door and step out onto the balcony. The fog has lifted. Below on the street, two yellow paramedic trucks sit at an angle on Riverview Drive along with half a dozen police cruisers. A large four-by-four truck has skidded into the lawn in front of the building, and the driver is standing on the lawn surrounded by several officers. Crowds gather along the sidewalk. Several road flares flicker bright and red, spilling white ash onto the asphalt around the scene.

Papers ruffle on the street, stuck in the damp ground with edges fluttering in a cold breeze that

vaults up from the swollen river. A blue backpack lies in the road, one with a yellow smiley face that faces me, glowing from the surrounding vehicles' lights. I suck in a lungful of cold, wet air. *My backpack.*

A group of paramedics surround a man crumpled on the street below. A sharp pain shoots up from my leg, coursing through my pelvis and up to my chest.

"You see, Kurt. It's over." Tyler stands in the open doorway. "Come back inside with me."

I lean against the balcony rail, nausea building in my stomach as my leg shakes with pain. "What is going on?"

> **"THINGS ARE NOT AS COMPREHENSIBLE AND EXPRESSIBLE AS PEOPLE USUALLY BELIEVE; WORKS OF ART ESPECIALLY LIVE IN A REALM BEYOND OUR CONFIDENT WORDS."**
> — RAINER MARIA RILKE

Tyler leans over me and touches my chin, lifting my head to look at him. "I can take it all away."

The pain and nausea vanish. The chill breeze halts as the lights below stop their flicker, frozen at a burst of red while the noise silences.

The shadow figure is standing next to me at the rail. But it isn't a shadow any longer. I can see features emerge of a head with dark hair, an arm holding a whiskey glass, and a white robe. Steven Belmonte. He is still as a statue, looking down at the scene below.

I follow his gaze. Everything has stopped moving, frozen like an image on a canvas. But I know who the man on the street is. I turn to Tyler. "*You* led me into traffic! So *that* would happen?"

Tyler's smile is sharp. "So we could be together again, like you wanted." Tyler grabs my hand. "Just stay here a few more moments, and the pain will never come back. It will be just you and me, the way it always should have been."

I glance at Steven Belmonte, who wears a robe just like I had earlier. A robe inscribed over the heart with scripted red letters. *Tyler's.* The cool weight of the pendant flutters against my chest.

I pull my hand away from Tyler. "No."

The air around us comes alive with voices from below. The red and blue lights flicker from the emergency vehicles, the sound of chatter over radios and urgent cries from the paramedics. "Losing him," a deep female voice shouts.

"Don't do this to me, Kurt!" Tyler cries. His fingers grasp for the chain around my neck.

I can't get around him. I hop onto the balcony rail, my feet slipping on the cold steel. Tyler grabs my arm, and I pull away fast, losing my balance before I fall backward.

My last sight of the balcony is of Steven Belmonte looking at me and Tyler, his face pale and mouth agape, punctuated by a sharp shattering trill as he drops his glass.

I fall, expecting a hard crack as my body meets the ground below. But that doesn't happen. Instead, I fall gently onto the grass, as if I was a weightless feather. I stand up and try to ignore the wails of Tyler above, begging my return.

I walk to the scene in the street. No one notices me as I walk, naked, past the observing crowds and into the thick of emergency personnel. A group of men and women surround my body. My cut-off clothes lie in a mangled pile where they had thrown them, and my body lies naked and bloodied on the road. My right leg is twisted, like a fleshy swizzle stick, and my pelvis is angled unnaturally to the left from my upper torso. My form on the road still wears my half of the Mizpah pendant Pete gave me, its gold shimmering against the harsh white lights placed around the scene. *Watch me and thee, we are absent another.* I kneel beside my body and take my own hand.

"He's in fib! AED, stat," someone shouts. A medic reaches to my body's pendant and tears it away. A medic places pads from a red and white case on my chest, shouts for everyone to back off and yells, "Clear!"

My body's chest rises and falls, my entire form shivering from the electric current. I feel it run up my arm and through me as my vision fades. Above, I can still hear Tyler wailing for me, his voice melding with my own as I lie on the asphalt, my world a cacophony of pain and screaming.

"He's awake!" someone cries out. I feel a prick in my arm and fall into darkness.

* * *

I don't know how many days I fade in and out at the hospital. Waking involves rhythms of pain assaulting my right side, from my toes up to my chest. If I say anything intelligible, I don't recall it. Just a lot of groaning and crying. At one point a doctor, a man with thinning gray hair and black-rimmed glasses tells me that landing on my stuffed backpack was all that saved my head from cracking against the asphalt like an egg and spilling my brains, not to mention sparing my spine. I have a cracked pelvis and badly damaged right leg, its shattered bone hooked back together with pins and wires, suspended above the bed for traction with metal rods inserted through the bones around my knee.

Lisa came by while I was sleeping. She found Pete's half of the Mizpah coin and left it for me. When I see it, I have the nurse hang it from the sling around my leg. Both our halves are together again.

Steven Belmonte visits me after my third week. He holds a drawing pad open to a sketch of Tyler. The very sketch I had drawn, signed and dated on the night I ended up in the hospital.

"I don't know how this is possible," he says, "but I found this on the coffee table after..." He pauses, his eyes roving over my suspended leg. "After I saw you that night on the balcony. With him."

"Yeah, I don't understand it, either." I look him in the eye, making an effort not to look at the sketch.

"When I saw the accident below, I thought of him. I thought that was why I saw him that night." He looks at the sketching pad. "But this I couldn't figure out."

I ask him to sit on the chair next to my bed and then ponder if I want to know the answer to a question that has been on my mind since that night. The words spill out before I can stop them. "Tell me what happened to him."

"I asked him to leave," he says, looking at the floor. "A year ago. Not to get into the details, but he was hooking up with guys behind my back."

I nod. "He used to tell me, 'Variety is the spice of life.'"

Steven scoffs. "Yeah, I heard that at least once. I told him his looks wouldn't serve him forever, and he had a nasty attitude after that. Pretty much just leeching off me while painting idealized versions of his past. He didn't even try to sell anything after a few prospects I set up turned him down. I wanted him gone." He flinches. "But not like this."

He pauses, looks at the sketch again, and then turns it face-down in his lap. "I had the locks changed when he was away, probably out hooking up again. He screamed at me from the lawn and, as I was watching him from the balcony, got this weird smile and walked into traffic. Gone instantly."

"Shit." That was dramatic even for Tyler, and I wonder if I ever really knew him. I look into Steven's pained face. "You didn't deserve that."

He looks at the floor. "Yeah, well…" His voice drifts off.

"Let me tell you about the night I made that sketch." He looks at me and, after a brief pause, nods. I tell him my story of that night at the condo, every detail I can remember.

When I finish, he leans back in the chair. "I sometimes see him standing in the shadows, just for a moment, feeling his anger and bitterness, and I get this onslaught of *guilt*. I dismissed it as my grief acting up, but it's so vivid. Feeling responsible for him, more than once I considered ending things for myself."

"Yeah," I say. "He has that way about him. *Had*, I mean."

"No, *has* is right." He holds up the sketch I made of Tyler. This time, I don't look away. The drawing's face has changed, holding a smirk, a mischievous sneer, just a hair more sinister than the Mona Lisa smile I considered drawing on him that night. "It changes, sometimes," Steven says. "Today, the smile is just like the one he had when he walked in front of that bus."

> **"NOTHING IN THIS WORLD IS HARDER THAN TELLING THE TRUTH, AND NOTHING EASIER THAN FLATTERY; YET ONLY TRUTH LETS A HUMAN BEING STAND UPRIGHT IN REALITY."**
>
> **— FYODOR DOSTOEVSKY**

"Burn it." A razor of animosity cuts through my voice, and it feels good. "Then burn all his paintings, everything. No good can come from them."

Steven closes the sketch pad and, after wishing me well, leaves with it. I hope he listens to me and does what I asked.

Part of me feels badly for Tyler, but I push it away. My leg is in painful pieces because of him, my body altered forever. It will be months of rehabilitation before I'll be able to walk again, and even then, I will probably have a permanent limp. Beyond the physical hardship, I have no insurance and will be paying for my recovery all my life. I begin to cry, which hurts because it shakes my suspended leg.

But at least you have a life. I imagine Pete's voice is saying it to me. The gold Mizpah coin shimmers as the halves jingle from where they hang. *May the Lord watch between me and thee while we are absent one from the other.* I'm not a religious person, but I appreciate the sentiment. I memorized the entire phrase ages ago, and in my mind, I often hear it whispered to me in Pete's voice. He was with me that night. I choose to believe he still is.

GUARD RAILS

BY **LARK ROWEN**
EDITED BY KALLISTA FOOTE

Gasoline, cedar, snow—the smells snap me back into consciousness.

The cold chases down my throat.

My back pressed against my seat like an astronaut launching toward the stars in a crumpled capsule, I list to the right against my seatbelt. The steering wheel pins the high bump of my belly. Snow speckles the windshield between the steady whir-thud of the wipers. The engine ticks, and steam hisses from the crack along the hood. A splintered branch skewers the passenger window, ending just inches from my face. Its solid trunk fills the view on that side. Tiny glass pebbles fall from my hair when I shift my gaze. Other branches pierce the car at odd angles along the right side.

Pain gnaws at my arm when I shove my door. I push harder, fighting gravity and gnarled metal before relenting.

My fingers wrestle into a pocket. I ease my phone out, catching a glimpse in the screen's reflection. Fading yellow bruises. New scuffs. Blood.

When the screen lights, I expel a breath. My eyes fill, and then I stare, rechecking the signal. I shake my head and lift the phone. Nausea undulates. The phone clatters free as I refocus.

Above, light sweeps the darkness and settles. Quintin's truck glides to a stop. My heart cannons into my aching ribs. The bang of his door carries down the distant swath I plowed.

My eyes cut to the rear seat and back. Quintin leans over the broken guard rail, crowbar clasped in his gloved hand, staring down at the wreckage around me. I swear his eyes lock with mine. He throws a leg over the railing and starts easing his way down the slope.

ILLUSTRATION BY SASHA DAVYDOVA

A low whimper spills from me. I renew the fight against my metal cage. I thrash and groan until my shaking fingers discover and unclip my seatbelt. I clamber-fall down into the back seat before squirming my way around branches toward the trunk.

Through the shattered rear window, I look back. Quintin is halfway down the slope. He sinks into the drifts up to his knees. His arms flail, and then he buries the crowbar like an icepick, breaking his slide.

My parka catches on the last branch.

Quintin slides closer.

I wriggle out of the coat and squeeze sideways between the empty window and ragged branch.

Quintin starts across the snowy impact craters my car made in its careening roll into the treetops.

Snow needles my face as I half drop, half slide down the car trunk. I buckle as I hit the ground, sinking into icy fuel-contaminated slush. My feet pedal and skid for purchase.

I turn and wade-run deeper into the woods through the snow. Arms wide, I pitch and sway, snagging against barren twigs and deadfall branches while sinking through the drifts.

I keep twisting back to check. Quintin doesn't rush. He navigates my narrow wake, constantly calling after me. I forge on, ignoring his pleas.

Ahead, the trees yield to open sky. My lungs burn, and my skin tightens against the whipping wind.

I gasp as the ground falls away to a dizzying ravine. My arms windmill. I wobble. Far below, flecks of white water cap the steel thread of a river.

I scan left and right, powder-mouthed.

Behind me snow crushes underfoot. My stomach churns as I spin to face him.

Quintin glowers. His fingers tighten around the crowbar.

I retreat another shuffled step. Stones trickle away under my boot heel. The wind scours my hair across my sight as silent tears freeze on my cheeks.

Teetering, I weigh the fall before meeting his gaze.

"Angela, stop it." With a slow shake of his head, he lowers the crowbar and extends his hand. His lips curl. "You lost control. Slid off the road."

"That's not what happened," I whisper. Blood whooshes in my ears like an ultrasound echo of that tiniest heartbeat. I cradle my stretched belly.

His stare bores into me, pinning me down. He reaches for me. "Please," he says. "Come back with me."

I sink to my knees. Then my hands.

A single held breath stops time.

My palm closes around a loose rock.

A trace of warmth crosses my cheek. His breath. His face leans in, close enough above his offered hand. My cry is guttural, primal, instant. I hurl my weighted fist, the rock cold and sharp, buried in my palm. It connects, the sound like a branch snapping. Quintin drops sideways past me. The crowbar clangs as it falls free, striking and bouncing over the ledge.

I recoil. My fingers spread in the snow and ice. I stagger to my feet. Quintin clamps my ankle. I scream. He stumbles up and steps toward me. I slip, pitching forward. My face strikes the ground. My lip splits against my teeth as I flail. My boot crunches into something solid. His fingers clasp my calf. I thrash and twist, crying too hard to see. Another wild kick—a howl—my anchor is gone.

Quintin is gone.

I tremble and pant, lying curled on the ground. The air is still, feathered with falling snow. I push up and lean on my hip, propping myself on my arm. One frozen hand cups my round belly. The hand I'm leaning on still clutches the rock. I stare at the smear of dark red on its cold grey planes. Then I look across the monochrome landscape beyond the ravine. An indifferent sky sends fat snowflakes pinwheeling into my hair and face.

I turn my numb gaze back toward the woods. A faint flicker of distant blue strobes through the darkened trunks. I pitch the bloodied rock over the edge and stand.

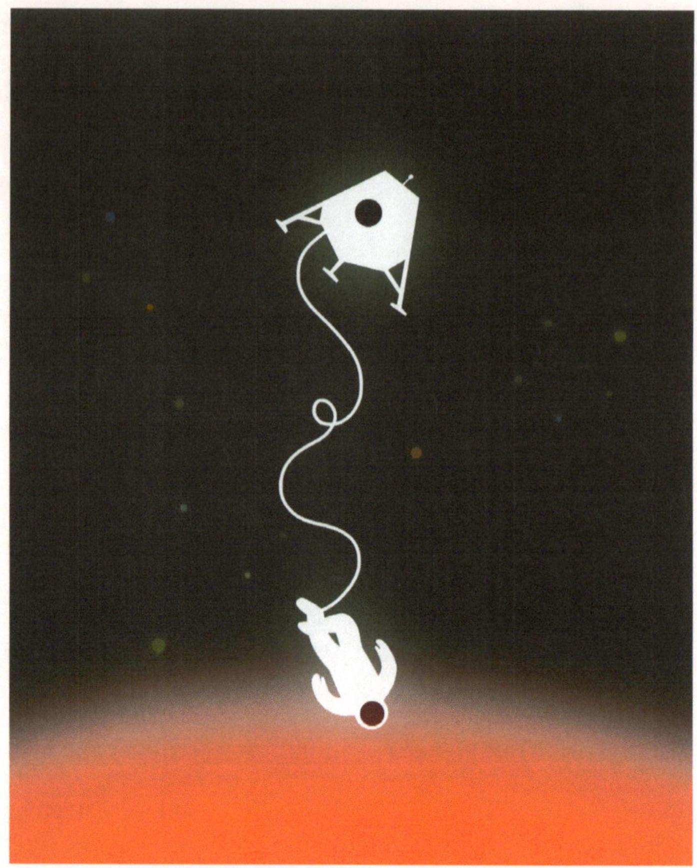

ESCALADE

BY **MARY KOEHLER**
EDITED BY JOANNE HAINES

I rolled the window down. The air hit wet and green—cut grass, exhaust, the river somewhere below. I closed my eyes and let it take my face.

David's elbow found my arm. The joint glowed between his fingers, trailing smoke that smelled like skunk and burnt cotton candy.

I waved him off. "I'm good."

He nodded, his eyes already closing, head ticking side to side. The bass thudded through the seat, through my spine.

Up front, Julie howled at something Bethany said. I'd missed it, didn't matter. "Stop," Julie gasped. "I'm gonna pee."

David leaned between the seats and killed the volume. "You piss in my Jeep, you're paying to clean it."

They shrieked. David dropped back beside me, grinning.

The world jerked forward. My chest hit the seatbelt. A single headlight, dead center. Glass sang. Then white. Then nothing—just cotton silence and my hands floating somewhere I couldn't see.

Something tugged at my shoulder. Sound came back in pieces—a voice, urgent, far away. Then closer. "Wake up. We gotta go." David's face, hovering. The door was open. When did that happen?

I tried to sit up. My body moved in pieces, delayed, like I was underwater.

"What..." My voice sounded wrong. Thick. "Where are we?"

ARTWORK BY SONNIE KOZLOVER

David's hands were under my arms, hauling. My feet found pavement. The world tilted and then steadied.

I looked at my hands. Scraped. No blood. I patted my chest, my legs. Everything moved. Everything hurt, but nothing screamed.

My fingers found my scalp. A lump the size of half an egg, pulsing.

The Jeep sat crooked in the road. The front end was gone—crumpled around twisted metal, a motorcycle folded into the wreckage like something swallowed. Chrome and fiberglass and a shattered wheel jutting sideways. "Bethany." The name left me before I knew I was speaking. "Julie." I lunged for the driver's door.

David's arm caught mine, shoved me back. "We gotta go." His voice was cracked open. He wasn't looking at me. He was looking at the car.

"No..." I reached past him. "Help me. We have to..."

His fingers dug into my arm. "We can't be here." His breath was short, ragged. "The cops. You think about what happens when they get here?"

"We have to help..." I twisted free.

"Help how?" David's voice broke. "Look at them."

I stepped to the window. I didn't want to. My body moved anyway.

Something was wrong with Bethany's face. Metal. There was metal in her face. Her mouth was open. Her eyes were open. She was looking at something in the windshield—a shape, a helmet, a head inside it, wrong, cracked like an egg, and I couldn't... I looked away. Looked back. It didn't change.

Julie wasn't moving. She was folded over the wheel, her arms hanging. Her hair—blonde, she had blonde hair—it wasn't blonde anymore.

A sound came out of me. I stepped back and hit David.

My stomach came up. I bent double and let it go—onto the pavement, onto my shoes. David scrambled back.

I spat, wiped my mouth on my sleeve. Straightened. "It's your dad's car. They'll know you were here."

"Julie took my keys. Julie took the car." He was talking fast now. "Nobody saw us get in."

"A BOOK MUST BE THE AXE FOR THE FROZEN SEA INSIDE US."
— FRANZ KAFKA

"So we just—what? We were never here?"

"If we were here, we lose everything." He ticked it off—my scholarship, his internship. "All of it. Gone." His voice steadied. Hardened. "And she was the one driving. Coked out of her mind."

"From your coke!" The words ripped out of me. My throat burned.

I turned away from him. From the car. The sky was clear. Stars. "Wake up," I said. To no one. To myself. "Wake up, wake up, wake up."

I pressed the heels of my hands into my eyes until I saw colors. Pulled them away.

David hadn't moved. Behind him, light swept across the road. Headlights. Coming closer.

The Escalade rolled up slowly. Black, massive. It stopped close enough that I could feel the engine idling in my chest.

The rear window slid down. A shape inside, no face I could see. "Get in." Not a request.

David exhaled. He still wasn't looking at me. "I called him. Right after." He walked toward the car.

I looked down. My shoes. Vomit on my shoes. The headlights caught the puddle. In it, upside down and shimmering, the Jeep. The shape in the windshield. I looked away.

"Ben." David's voice. Not a question.

I looked back. Julie's hair. Bethany's open mouth. The helmet between them.

"I'm sorry."

Then I walked to the car.

THE MONKEY'S PAW

BY W.W. JACOBS

EDITED BY HENRY ALDEN MILLS

Harper's Magazine, September 1902, (vol. CV, no. DCXXVIII)

I.

Without, the night was cold and wet, but in the small parlour of Laburnam Villa the blinds were drawn and the fire burned brightly. Father and son were at chess, the former, who possessed ideas about the game involving radical changes, putting his king into such sharp and unnecessary perils that it even provoked comment from the white-haired old lady knitting placidly by the fire.

"Hark at the wind," said Mr. White, who, having seen a fatal mistake after it was too late, was amiably desirous of preventing his son from seeing it.

"I'm listening," said the latter, grimly surveying the board as he stretched out his hand. "Check."

"I should hardly think that he'd come tonight," said his father, with his hand poised over the board.

"Mate," replied the son.

ILLUSTRATION BY HUNTER KEENE

"That's the worst of living so far out," bawled Mr. White, with sudden and unlooked-for violence; "of all the beastly, slushy, out-of-the-way places to live in, this is the worst. Pathway's a bog, and the road's a torrent. I don't know what people are thinking about. I suppose because only two houses in the road are let, they think it doesn't matter."

"Never mind, dear," said his wife, soothingly; "perhaps you'll win the next one."

Mr. White looked up sharply, just in time to intercept a knowing glance between mother and son. The words died away on his lips, and he hid a guilty grin in his thin grey beard.

"There he is," said Herbert White, as the gate banged to loudly and heavy footsteps came toward the door.

The old man rose with hospitable haste, and opening the door, was heard condoling with the new arrival. The new arrival also condoled with himself, so that Mrs. White said, "Tut, tut!" and coughed gently as her husband entered the room, followed by a tall, burly man, beady of eye and rubicund of visage.

"Sergeant-Major Morris," he said, introducing him.

The sergeant-major shook hands, and taking the proffered seat by the fire, watched contentedly while his host got out whiskey and tumblers and stood a small copper kettle on the fire.

At the third glass his eyes got brighter, and he began to talk, the little family circle regarding with eager interest this visitor from distant parts, as he squared his broad shoulders in the chair and spoke of wild scenes and doughty deeds; of wars and plagues and strange peoples.

"Twenty-one years of it," said Mr. White, nodding at his wife and son. "When he went away he was a slip of a youth in the warehouse. Now look at him."

"He don't look to have taken much harm," said Mrs. White, politely.

"I'd like to go to India myself," said the old man, "just to look round a bit, you know."

"Better where you are," said the sergeant-major, shaking his head. He put down the empty glass, and sighing softly, shook it again.

"I should like to see those old temples and fakirs and jugglers," said the old man. "What was that you started telling me the other day about a monkey's paw or something, Morris?"

"Nothing," said the soldier, hastily. "Leastways nothing worth hearing."

"Monkey's paw?" said Mrs. White, curiously.

"Well, it's just a bit of what you might call magic, perhaps," said the sergeant-major, offhandedly.

His three listeners leaned forward eagerly. The visitor absent-mindedly put his empty glass to his lips and then set it down again. His host filled it for him.

"To look at," said the sergeant-major, fumbling in his pocket, "it's just an ordinary little paw, dried to a mummy."

He took something out of his pocket and proffered it. Mrs. White drew back with a grimace, but her son, taking it, examined it curiously.

"And what is there special about it?" inquired Mr. White as he took it from his son, and having examined it, placed it upon the table.

"It had a spell put on it by an old fakir," said the sergeant-major, "a very holy man. He wanted to show that fate ruled people's lives, and that those who interfered with it did so to their sorrow. He put a spell on it so that three separate men could each have three wishes from it."

His manner was so impressive that his hearers were conscious that their light laughter jarred somewhat.

"Well, why don't you have three, sir?" said Herbert White, cleverly.

The soldier regarded him in the way that middle age is wont to regard presumptuous youth. "I have," he said, quietly, and his blotchy face whitened.

"And did you really have the three wishes granted?" asked Mrs. White.

"I did," said the sergeant-major, and his glass tapped against his strong teeth.

"And has anybody else wished?" persisted the old lady.

"The first man had his three wishes. Yes," was the reply; "I don't know what the first two were, but the third was for death. That's how I got the paw."

His tones were so grave that a hush fell upon the group.

"If you've had your three wishes, it's no good to you now, then, Morris," said the old man at last. "What do you keep it for?"

The soldier shook his head. "Fancy, I suppose," he said, slowly. "I did have some idea of selling it, but I don't think I will. It has caused enough mischief already. Besides, people won't buy. They think it's a fairy tale; some of them, and those who do think anything of it want to try it first and pay me afterward."

"If you could have another three wishes," said the old man, eyeing him keenly, "would you have them?"

"I don't know," said the other. "I don't know."

He took the paw, and dangling it between his forefinger and thumb, suddenly threw it upon the fire. White, with a slight cry, stooped down and snatched it off.

"Better let it burn," said the soldier, solemnly.

"If you don't want it, Morris," said the other, "give it to me."

"I won't," said his friend, doggedly. "I threw it on the fire. If you keep it, don't blame me for what happens. Pitch it on the fire again like a sensible man."

The other shook his head and examined his new possession closely. "How do you do it?" he inquired.

"Hold it up in your right hand and wish aloud," said the sergeant-major, "but I warn you of the consequences."

"Sounds like the Arabian Nights," said Mrs. White, as she rose and began to set the supper. "Don't you think you might wish for four pairs of hands for me?"

Her husband drew the talisman from his pocket, and then all three burst into laughter as the sergeant-major, with a look of alarm on his face, caught him by the arm.

"If you must wish," he said, gruffly, "wish for something sensible."

Mr. White dropped it back in his pocket and, placing chairs, motioned his friend to the table. In the business of supper the talisman was partly forgotten, and afterward the three sat listening in an enthralled fashion to a second instalment of the soldier's adventures in India.

"If the tale about the monkey's paw is not more truthful than those he has been telling us," said Herbert, as the door closed behind their guest, just in time for him to catch the last train, "we sha'nt make much out of it."

"Did you give him anything for it, Father?" inquired Mrs. White, regarding her husband closely.

"A trifle," said he, colouring slightly. "He didn't want it, but I made him take it. And he pressed me again to throw it away."

"Likely," said Herbert, with pretended horror. "Why, we're going to be rich, and famous and happy. Wish to be an emperor, Father, to begin with; then you can't be henpecked."

He darted round the table, pursued by the maligned Mrs. White armed with an antimacassar.

Mr. White took the paw from his pocket and eyed it dubiously. "I don't know what to wish for, and that's a fact," he said, slowly. "It seems to me I've got all I want."

"If you only cleared the house, you'd be quite happy, wouldn't you?" said Herbert, with his hand on his shoulder. "Well, wish for two hundred pounds, then; that'll just do it."

His father, smiling shamefacedly at his own credulity, held up the talisman, as his son, with a solemn face, somewhat marred by a wink at his mother, sat down at the piano and struck a few impressive chords.

"I wish for two hundred pounds," said the old man distinctly.

A fine crash from the piano greeted the words, interrupted by a shuddering cry from the old man. His wife and son ran toward him.

"It moved," he cried, with a glance of disgust at the object as it lay on the floor.

"As I wished, it twisted in my hand like a snake."

"Well, I don't see the money," said his son as he picked it up and placed it on the table, "and I bet I never shall."

"It must have been your fancy, Father," said his wife, regarding him anxiously.

He shook his head. "Never mind, though; there's no harm done, but it gave me a shock all the same."

They sat down by the fire again while the two men finished their pipes. Outside, the wind was higher than ever, and the old man started nervously at the sound of a door banging upstairs. A silence unusual and depressing settled upon all three, which lasted until the old couple rose to retire for the night.

"I expect you'll find the cash tied up in a big bag in the middle of your bed," said Herbert, as he bade them good-night, "and something horrible squatting up on top of the wardrobe watching you as you pocket your ill-gotten gains."

He sat alone in the darkness, gazing at the dying fire, and seeing faces in it. The last face was so horrible and so simian that he gazed at it in amazement. It got so vivid that, with a little uneasy laugh, he felt on the table for a glass containing a little water to throw over it. His hand grasped the monkey's paw, and with a little shiver he wiped his hand on his coat and went up to bed.

II.

In the brightness of the wintry sun next morning as it streamed over the breakfast table he laughed at his fears. There was an air of prosaic wholesomeness about the room which it had lacked on the previous night, and the dirty, shrivelled little paw was pitched on the sideboard with a carelessness which betokened no great belief in its virtues.

"I suppose all old soldiers are the same," said Mrs. White. "The idea of our listening to such nonsense! How could wishes be granted in these days? And if they could, how could two hundred pounds hurt you, Father?"

"Might drop on his head from the sky," said the frivolous Herbert.

"Morris said the things happened so naturally," said his father, "that you might if you so wished attribute it to coincidence."

"Well, don't break into the money before I come back," said Herbert as he rose from the table. "I'm afraid it'll turn you into a mean, avaricious man, and we shall have to disown you."

His mother laughed, and following him to the door, watched him down the road; and returning to the breakfast table, was very happy at the expense of her husband's credulity. All of which did not prevent her from scurrying to the door at the postman's knock, nor prevent her from referring somewhat shortly to retired sergeant-majors of bibulous habits when she found that the post brought a tailor's bill.

"Herbert will have some more of his funny remarks, I expect, when he comes home," she said, as they sat at dinner.

"I dare say," said Mr. White, pouring himself out some beer; "but for all that, the thing moved in my hand; that I'll swear to."

"You thought it did," said the old lady soothingly.

"I say it did," replied the other. "There was no thought about it; I had just… What's the matter?"

His wife made no reply. She was watching the mysterious movements of a man outside, who, peering in an undecided fashion at the house, appeared to be trying to make up his mind to enter. In mental connection with the two hundred pounds, she noticed that the stranger was well dressed, and wore a silk hat of glossy newness. Three times he paused at the gate, and then walked on again. The fourth time he stood with his hand upon it, and then with sudden resolution flung it open and walked up the path. Mrs. White at the same moment placed her hands behind her and, hurriedly unfastening the strings of her apron, put that useful article of apparel beneath the cushion of her chair.

She brought the stranger, who seemed ill at ease, into the room. He gazed at her furtively, and listened in a preoccupied fashion as the old lady apologized for the appearance of the room, and her husband's coat, a garment which he usually reserved for the garden. She then waited as patiently as her sex would permit, for him to broach his business, but he was at first strangely silent.

"I—was asked to call," he said at last, and stooped and picked a piece of cotton from his trousers. "I come from 'Maw and Meggins.'"

The old lady started. "Is anything the matter?" she asked, breathlessly. "Has anything happened to Herbert? What is it? What is it?"

Her husband interposed. "There, there, Mother," he said, hastily. "Sit down, and don't jump to conclusions. You've not brought bad news, I'm sure, sir;" and he eyed the other wistfully.

"I'm sorry—" began the visitor.

"Is he hurt?" demanded the mother, wildly.

The visitor bowed in assent. "Badly hurt," he said, quietly, "but he is not in any pain."

"Oh, thank God!" said the old woman, clasping her hands. "Thank God for that! Thank—"

She broke off suddenly as the sinister meaning of the assurance dawned upon her and she saw the awful confirmation of her fears in the other's averted face. She caught her breath and, turning to her slower-witted husband, laid her trembling old hand upon his. There was a long silence.

"He was caught in the machinery," said the visitor at length in a low voice.

"Caught in the machinery," repeated Mr. White, in a dazed fashion, "yes."

He sat staring blankly out at the window, and taking his wife's hand between his own, pressed it as he had been wont to do in their old courting-days nearly forty years before.

"He was the only one left to us," he said, turning gently to the visitor. "It is hard."

The other coughed and, rising, walked slowly to the window. "The firm wished me to convey their sincere sympathy with you in your great loss," he said, without looking round. "I beg that you will understand I am only their servant and merely obeying orders."

There was no reply; the old woman's face was white, her eyes staring, and her breath inaudible; on the husband's face was a look such as his friend the sergeant might have carried into his first action.

"I was to say that 'Maw and Meggins' disclaim all responsibility," continued the other. "They admit no liability at all, but in consideration of your son's services, they wish to present you with a certain sum as compensation."

Mr. White dropped his wife's hand and, rising to his feet, gazed with a look of horror at his visitor. His dry lips shaped the words, "How much?"

"Two hundred pounds," was the answer.

Unconscious of his wife's shriek, the old man smiled faintly, put out his hands like a sightless man, and dropped, a senseless heap, to the floor.

III.

In the huge new cemetery, some two miles distant, the old people buried their dead, and came back to a house steeped in shadow and silence. It was all over so quickly that at first they could hardly realize it, and remained in a state of expectation as though of something else to happen—something else which was to lighten this load, too heavy for old hearts to bear.

But the days passed, and expectation gave place to resignation—the hopeless resignation of the old, sometimes miscalled, apathy. Sometimes they hardly exchanged a word, for now they had nothing to talk about, and their days were long to weariness.

It was about a week after that the old man, waking suddenly in the night, stretched out his hand and found himself alone. The room was in darkness, and the sound of subdued weeping came from the window. He raised himself in bed and listened.

"Come back," he said, tenderly. "You will be cold."

"It is colder for my son," said the old woman, and wept afresh.

The sound of her sobs died away on his ears. The bed was warm, and his eyes heavy with sleep. He dozed fitfully, and then slept until a sudden wild cry from his wife awoke him with a start.

FIX THE PAST

CHO

SCOTT SMITH'S CLASSIC
MEETS H.G. WELLS'S SEMINAL SCIENCE

"The paw!" she cried wildly. "The monkey's paw!"

He started up in alarm. "Where? Where is it? What's the matter?"

She came stumbling across the room toward him. "I want it," she said, quietly. "You've not destroyed it?"

"It's in the parlour, on the bracket," he replied, marvelling. "Why?"

She cried and laughed together, and bending over, kissed his cheek.

"I only just thought of it," she said, hysterically. "Why didn't I think of it before? Why didn't you think of it?"

"Think of what?" he questioned.

"The other two wishes," she replied, rapidly. "We've only had one."

"Was not that enough?" he demanded, fiercely.

"No," she cried, triumphantly; "we'll have one more. Go down and get it quickly, and wish our boy alive again."

The man sat up in bed and flung the bedclothes from his quaking limbs. "Good God, you are mad!" he cried, aghast.

"Get it," she panted; "get it quickly, and wish— Oh, my boy, my boy!"

Her husband struck a match and lit the candle. "Get back to bed," he said, unsteadily. "You don't know what you are saying."

"We had the first wish granted," said the old woman, feverishly; "why not the second?"

"A coincidence," stammered the old man.

"Go and get it and wish," cried his wife, quivering with excitement.

The old man turned and regarded her, and his voice shook. "He has been dead ten days, and besides he—I would not tell you else, but—I could only recognize him by his clothing. If he was too terrible for you to see then, how now?"

"Bring him back," cried the old woman, and dragged him toward the door. "Do you think I fear the child I have nursed?"

He went down in the darkness, and felt his way to the parlour, and then to the mantelpiece. The talisman was in its place, and a horrible fear that the unspoken wish might bring his mutilated son before him ere he could escape from the room seized upon him, and he caught his breath as he found that he had lost the direction of the door. His brow cold with sweat, he felt his way round the table, and groped along the wall until he found himself in the small passage with the unwholesome thing in his hand.

Even his wife's face seemed changed as he entered the room. It was white and expectant, and to his fears seemed to have an unnatural look upon it. He was afraid of her.

"Wish!" she cried, in a strong voice.

"It is foolish and wicked," he faltered.

"Wish!" repeated his wife.

He raised his hand. "I wish my son alive again."

The talisman fell to the floor, and he regarded it fearfully. Then he sank trembling into a chair as the old woman, with burning eyes, walked to the window and raised the blind.

He sat until he was chilled with the cold, glancing occasionally at the figure of the old woman peering through the window. The candle-end, which had burned below the rim of the china candlestick, was throwing pulsating shadows on the ceiling and walls, until, with a flicker larger than the rest, it expired. The old man, with an unspeakable sense of relief at the failure of the talisman, crept back to his bed, and a minute or two afterward the old woman came silently and apathetically beside him.

Neither spoke, but lay silently listening to the ticking of the clock. A stair creaked, and a squeaky mouse scurried noisily through the wall. The darkness was oppressive, and after lying for some time screwing up his courage, he took the box of matches, and striking one, went downstairs for a candle.

At the foot of the stairs the match went out, and he paused to strike another; and at the same moment a knock, so quiet and stealthy as to be scarcely audible, sounded on the front door.

The matches fell from his hand and spilled in the passage. He stood motionless, his breath suspended until the knock was repeated. Then he turned and fled swiftly back to his room, and closed the door behind him. A third knock sounded through the house.

"What's that?" cried the old woman, starting up.

"A rat," said the old man in shaking tones. "A rat. It passed me on the stairs."

His wife sat up in bed listening. A loud knock resounded through the house.

"It's Herbert!" she screamed. "It's Herbert!"

She ran to the door, but her husband was before her and, catching her by the arm, held her tightly.

"What are you going to do?" he whispered hoarsely.

"It's my boy; it's Herbert!" she cried, struggling mechanically. "I forgot it was two miles away. What are you holding me for? Let go. I must open the door."

"For God's sake don't let it in," cried the old man, trembling.

"You're afraid of your own son," she cried, struggling. "Let me go. I'm coming, Herbert; I'm coming."

There was another knock, and another. The old woman with a sudden wrench broke free and ran from the room. Her husband followed to the landing, and called after her appealingly as she hurried downstairs. He heard the chain rattle back and the bottom bolt drawn slowly and stiffly from the socket. Then the old woman's voice, strained and panting.

"The bolt," she cried, loudly. "Come down. I can't reach it."

But her husband was on his hands and knees groping wildly on the floor in search of the paw. If he could only find it before the thing outside got in. A perfect fusillade of knocks reverberated through the house, and he heard the scraping of a chair as his wife put it down in the passage against the door. He heard the creaking of the bolt as it came slowly back, and at the same moment he found the monkey's paw, and frantically breathed his third and last wish.

The knocking ceased suddenly, although the echoes of it were still in the house. He heard the chair drawn back, and the door opened. A cold wind rushed up the staircase, and a long loud wail of disappointment and misery from his wife gave him courage to run down to her side, and then to the gate beyond. The street lamp flickering opposite shone on a quiet and deserted road.

THE GAME

BY **RANDALL SURLES**
EDITED BY TIM GRAHL

The scarab catches the torchlight, gold flashing between my fingers. Lighter than it should be. I turn it over—smooth seam along the belly, plastic under the paint.

The torches flicker—tissue paper and LEDs, but the shadows move right, jumping across sandstone walls and a jackal-headed statue in the corner.

"One more number!" Lisa's voice bounces off the walls. She's bent over the pedestal, her fingers tracing the grid carved into its surface.

The hourglass in the center of the room is half my height. The sand has dropped past the red line—five minutes, maybe less. I weave around a sarcophagus, duck under a hanging ankh, and crouch beside her.

Lisa's fingers move across the grid, sliding tiles into place. Click. Click. Click.

"Fireplace numbers. Book of the Dead numbers. I've tried everything." Her jaw is tight.

I reach around her, find the forty-five tile, and slide it to the end of the row. It catches and then clicks into place.

"Under the carpet," I say.

The panel hums. Blue light floods up from the grid—blacklight. Suddenly the walls are alive with symbols that weren't there before, glowing violet and green.

Lisa lifts the panel. Underneath, resting in velvet: a key. Gold, heavy-looking, carved with tiny hieroglyphs.

"You're amazing." I'm still crouched beside her, close enough to smell her shampoo—coconut, something floral.

ARTWORK BY **KIMMY QUILLIN**

"Yet you keep shooting me down."

She laughs, half-turns—and the key slips. It hits the sand without a sound and vanishes.

"Shit." We drop. My hands plunge into the sand—coarse, deeper than it looks, still warm from the lights above.

My fingers find cold metal. "Got it."

She snatches it from my palm and bolts. The door at the far wall—the only one we haven't cracked.

I push up from the sand, brush off my knees. "Come on. I've got reservations at McCalebs. Tonight."

She tucks a strand of blonde hair behind her ear, her eyes on the lock. "You were serious about that?" The key slides in. She twists—click, click, click.

"I just ended it with Andrew." She doesn't turn around. "My therapist says I need to date myself for a while."

A voice shakes the walls—deep, theatrical, dripping with fake ancient menace. "Three minutes left. Can you escape the final crypt before I rise from my grave? Muahahahaha." The laugh that follows echoes too long, rattling in my chest.

The door shudders. Stone grinding against stone—or something made to sound like it. It swings inward, revealing darkness.

I catch the edge of the door, hold it wide. "You always have an excuse." She's already through the doorway. I follow. "Every time."

That's ridiculous." She's sizing up the coffin in the center of the room—black lacquer, fake jewels crusted along the edges. Her hands run across the lid, searching for a latch.

Bookshelves climb the walls on either side—leather spines, gold titles. Another door, dead ahead. Still closed.

"It's true." I drift toward the bookshelves, ticking fingers. "Hank in sophomore year." I pull a book spine. Nothing. "Dan and Tom last year. And that other short guy—whatshisname." Another spine. "The one who always smelled like garlic."

"Ron." She's moved to the far door, up on tiptoe, her fingers sweeping the top of the frame. Down the sides.

"No handle. Must be a trigger somewhere. Stop talking and start looking."

She's beside me before I register she moved. Close enough that our elbows bump. "I can't believe you mentioned Tom." She yanks a book. Nothing happens. She shoves it back.

I pull another book. Hold it. I'm not even looking at it.

"Look, Lisa." I slide the book back in. "You've friend-zoned me for four years." I turn to face her. "I can't do it anymore."

She turns back to the shelf. Pulls a book, shoves it back. Another. "Call out the titles. Could be a clue." Her voice is too bright. *"Death in Venice. Death on the Nile."*

She stops. The book stays in her hand. "Why aren't you reading out titles?"

"Because this is more important." I haven't moved. "I'm serious."

She slides the book back. Slow. Careful. "We're friends." Barely above a whisper.

"I want more than that."

Her shoulders rise. Fall.

"I mean, you're my only friend." She's looking at the shelf, not at me. "You don't judge. I can tell you everything."

Something loosens in my chest. "Sounds like dating material to me."

She laughs—short, surprised, almost against her will.

"Seriously, though." Somewhere behind us, sand is still falling. "If all these other guys are assholes, why won't you give me a chance?"

Her hands freeze on the bookshelf.

"That's the thing." Her voice is different now. Quiet. True. "You're the only one I don't want to risk losing."

The voice returns, oozing through the walls. "Two minutes remaining. Before eternal servitude begins!" The laugh again—too loud, too long.

I take her hands. She lets me. When I duck my head, she finally looks up.

"Lees, I can't keep doing this." Her hands are cold. "Showing up for you. Following you around like a lost puppy." I swallow. "Watching you fall for every guy who crosses your path. Every guy except me."

"That's not fair." She pulls her hands back.

"I agree." My voice doesn't sound like mine. "This is it for me."

Neither of us moves. The torches flicker. Somewhere, a hidden timer is counting down what we have left.

She looks away first. Steps back.

"We have to find the final code."

She crosses to the shelf, yanking books, shoving them back. Too fast. Too hard.

I close my eyes. Tip my head back. Let the breath go out of me.

"Aren't you going to help?"

"I don't think so."

"Come on. We'll miss our first date if we're stuck in here for eternity."

I open my eyes. She's stopped pulling books. She's looking at me—and there it is. The smallest smile. A dare.

"For real?"

A quick nod. Hair falls across her face, but not before I catch the shine in her eyes.

"Now come on." She turns back to the shelves, her voice thick. "We've got like thirty seconds."

Books fly off the shelf. She's not even looking at titles anymore.

"Lees." She turns. I point up.

There, on the ceiling, glowing white: DEATH IS MY EXIT STRATEGY.

"The sarcophagus!" She's already there.

I drop beside her, my hands running under the edge. There—a ridge, a button. I press it.

Something clicks. Gears grind. A bell explodes through the speakers—and then silence.

XINGU

BY EDITH WHARTON

EDITED BY EDWARD L. BURLINGAME

Scribner's Magazine, July–December 1911, (vol. L)

I

Mrs. Ballinger is one of the ladies who pursue Culture in bands, as though it were dangerous to meet alone. To this end she had founded the Lunch Club, an association composed of herself and several other indomitable huntresses of erudition. The Lunch Club, after three or four winters of lunching and debate, had acquired such local distinction that the entertainment of distinguished strangers became one of its accepted functions; in recognition of which it duly extended to the celebrated "Osric Dane," on the day of her arrival in Hillbridge, an invitation to be present at the next meeting.

ILLUSTRATION BY HUNTER KEENE

The club was to meet at Mrs. Bellinger's. The other members, behind her back, were of one voice in deploring her unwillingness to cede her rights in favor of Mrs. Plinth, whose house made a more impressive setting for the entertainment of celebrities; while, as Mrs. Leveret observed, there was always the picture-gallery to fall back on.

Mrs. Plinth made no secret of sharing this view. She had always regarded it as one of her obligations to entertain the Lunch Club's distinguished guests. Mrs. Plinth was almost as proud of her obligations as she was of her picture-gallery; she was in fact fond of implying that the one possession implied the other, and that only a woman of her wealth could afford to live up to a standard as high as that which she had set herself. An all-round sense of duty, roughly adaptable to various ends, was, in her opinion, all that Providence exacted of the more humbly stationed; but the power which had predestined Mrs. Plinth to keep a footman clearly intended her to maintain an equally specialized staff of responsibilities. It was the more to be regretted that Mrs. Ballinger, whose obligations to society were bounded by the narrow scope of two parlour-maids, should have been so tenacious of the right to entertain Osric Dane.

The question of that lady's reception had for a month past profoundly moved the members of the Lunch Club. It was not that they felt themselves unequal to the task, but that their sense of the opportunity plunged them into the agreeable uncertainty of the lady who weighs the alternatives of a well-stocked wardrobe. If such subsidiary members as Mrs. Leveret were fluttered by the thought of exchanging ideas with the author of "The Wings of Death," no forebodings disturbed the conscious adequacy of Mrs. Plinth, Mrs. Ballinger and Miss Van Vluyck. "The Wings of Death" had, in fact, at Miss Van Vluyck's suggestion, been chosen as the subject of discussion at the last club meeting, and each member had thus been enabled to express her own opinion or to appropriate whatever sounded well in the comments of the others.

Mrs. Roby alone had abstained from profiting by the opportunity; but it was now openly recognised that, as a member of the Lunch Club, Mrs. Roby was a failure. "It all comes," as Miss Van Vluyck put it, "of accepting a woman on a man's estimation." Mrs. Roby, returning to Hillbridge from a prolonged sojourn in exotic lands—the other ladies no longer took the trouble to remember where—had been heralded by the distinguished biologist, Professor Foreland, as the most agreeable woman he had ever met; and the members of the Lunch Club, impressed by an encomium that carried the weight of a diploma, and rashly assuming that the Professor's social sympathies would follow the line of his professional bent, had seized the chance of annexing a biological member. Their disillusionment was complete. At Miss Van Vluyck's first off-hand mention of the pterodactyl Mrs. Roby had confusedly murmured: "I know so little about metres—" and after that painful betrayal of incompetence she had prudently withdrawn from farther participation in the mental gymnastics of the club.

"I suppose she flattered him," Miss Van Vluyck summed up—"or else it's the way she does her hair."

The dimensions of Miss Van Vluyck's dining-room having restricted the membership of the club to six, the nonconductiveness of one member was a serious obstacle to the exchange of ideas, and some wonder had already been expressed that Mrs. Roby should care to live, as it were, on the intellectual bounty of the others. This feeling was increased by the discovery that she had not yet read "The Wings of Death." She owned to having heard the name of Osric Dane; but that—incredible as it appeared—was the extent of her acquaintance with the celebrated novelist. The ladies could not conceal their surprise; but Mrs. Ballinger, whose pride in the club made her wish to put even Mrs. Roby in the best possible light, gently insinuated that, though she had not had time to acquaint herself with "The Wings of Death," she must at least be familiar with its equally remarkable predecessor, "The Supreme Instant."

Mrs. Roby wrinkled her sunny brows in a conscientious effort of memory, as a result of which she recalled that, oh, yes, she *had* seen the book at her brother's, when she was staying with him in Brazil, and had even carried it off to read one day on a boating party; but they had all got to shying things at each other in the boat, and the book had gone overboard, so she had never had the chance—

The picture evoked by this anecdote did not increase Mrs. Roby's credit with the club, and there was a painful pause, which was broken by Mrs. Plinth's remarking:

"I can understand that, with all your other pursuits, you should not find much time for reading; but I should have thought you might at least have *got up* 'The Wings of Death' before Osric Dane's arrival."

Mrs. Roby took this rebuke good-humouredly. She had meant, she owned, to glance through the book; but she had been so absorbed in a novel of Trollope's that—

"No one reads Trollope now," Mrs. Ballinger interrupted.

Mrs. Roby looked pained. "I'm only just beginning," she confessed.

"And does he interest you?" Mrs. Plinth enquired.

"He amuses me."

"Amusement," said Mrs. Plinth, "is hardly what I look for in my choice of books."

"Oh, certainly, 'The Wings of Death' is not amusing," ventured Mrs. Leveret, whose manner of putting forth an opinion was like that of an obliging salesman with a variety of other styles to submit if his first selection does not suit.

"Was it *meant* to be?" enquired Mrs. Plinth, who was fond of asking questions that she permitted no one but herself to answer. "Assuredly not."

"Assuredly not—that is what I was going to say," assented Mrs. Leveret, hastily rolling up her opinion and reaching for another. "It was meant to—to elevate."

Miss Van Vluyck adjusted her spectacles as though they were the black cap of condemnation. "I hardly see," she interposed, "how a book steeped in the bitterest pessimism can be said to elevate however much it may instruct."

"I meant, of course, to instruct," said Mrs. Leveret, flurried by the unexpected distinction between two terms which she had supposed to be synonymous. Mrs. Leveret's enjoyment of the Lunch Club was frequently marred by such surprises; and not knowing her own value to the other ladies as a mirror for their mental complacency she was sometimes troubled by a doubt of her worthiness to join in their debates. It was only the fact of having a dull sister who thought her clever that saved her, from a sense of hopeless inferiority.

"Do they get married in the end?" Mrs. Roby interposed.

"They—who?" the Lunch Club collectively exclaimed.

"Why, the girl and man. It's a novel, isn't it? I always think that's the one thing that matters. If they're parted it spoils my dinner."

Mrs. Plinth and Mrs. Ballinger exchanged scandalised glances, and the latter said: "I should hardly advise you to read 'The Wings of Death' in that spirit. For my part, when there are so many books one *has* to read; I wonder how any one can find time for those that are merely amusing."

"The beautiful part of it," Laura Glyde murmured, "is surely just this—that no one can tell how 'The Wings of Death' ends. Osric Dane, overcome by the awful significance of her own meaning, has mercifully veiled it—perhaps even from herself—as Apelles, in representing the sacrifice of Iphigenia, veiled the face of Agamemnon."

"What's that? Is it poetry?" whispered Mrs. Leveret to Mrs. Plinth, who, disdaining a definite reply, said coldly: "You should look it up. I always make it a point to look things up." Her tone added—"though I might easily have it done for me by the footman."

"I was about to say," Miss Van Vluyck resumed, "that it must always be a question whether a book *can* instruct unless it elevates."

"Oh—" murmured Mrs. Leveret, now feeling herself hopelessly astray.

"I don't know," said Mrs. Ballinger, scenting in Miss Van Vluyck's tone a tendency to depreciate the coveted distinction of entertaining Osric Dane; "I don't know that such a question can seriously be raised as to a book which has attracted more attention among thoughtful people than any novel since 'Robert Elsmere.'"

"Oh, but don't you see," exclaimed Laura Glyde, "that it's just the dark hopelessness of it all—the wonderful tone-scheme of black on black—that makes it such an artistic achievement? It reminded me when I read it of Prince Rupert's *manière noire*...the book is etched, not painted, yet one feels the colour-values so intensely...."

"Who is he?" Mrs. Leveret whispered to her neighbour. "Some one she's met abroad?"

"The wonderful part of the book," Mrs. Bellinger conceded, "is that it may be looked at from so many points of view. I hear that as a study of determinism Professor Lupton ranks it with 'The Data of Ethics.'"

"I'm told that Osric Dane spent ten years in preparatory studies before beginning to write it," said Mrs. Plinth. "She looks up everything—verifies everything. It has always been my principle, as you know. Nothing would induce me, now, to put aside a book before I'd finished it, just because I can buy as many more as I want."

"And what do *you* think of 'The Wings of Death'?" Mrs. Roby abruptly asked her.

It was the kind of question that might be termed out of order, and the ladies glanced at each other as though disclaiming any share in such a breach of discipline. They all knew there was nothing Mrs. Plinth so much disliked as being asked her opinion of a book. Books were written to read; if one read them what more could be expected? To be questioned in detail regarding the contents of a volume seemed to her as great an outrage as being searched for smuggled laces at the Custom House. The club had always respected this idiosyncrasy of Mrs. Plinth's. Such opinions as she had were imposing and substantial: her mind, like her house, was furnished with monumental "pieces" that were not meant to be disarranged; and it was one of the unwritten rules of the Lunch Club that, within her own province, each member's habits of thought should be respected. The meeting therefore closed with an increased sense, on the part of the other ladies, of Mrs. Roby's hopeless unfitness to be one of them.

II

Mrs. Leveret, on the eventful day, arrived early at Mrs. Ballinger's, her volume of Appropriate Allusions in her pocket.

It always flustered Mrs. Leveret to be late at the Lunch Club: she liked to collect her thoughts and gather a hint, as the others assembled, of the turn the conversation was likely to take. To-day, however, she felt herself completely at a loss; and even the familiar contact of Appropriate Allusions, which stuck into her as she sat down, failed to give her any reassurance. It was an admirable little volume, compiled to meet all the social emergencies; so that, whether on the occasion of Anniversaries, joyful or melancholy (as the classification ran), of Banquets, social or municipal, or of Baptisms, Church of England or sectarian, its student need never be at a loss for a pertinent reference. Mrs. Leveret, though she had for years devoutly conned its pages, valued it, however, rather for its moral support than for its practical services; for though in the privacy of her own room she commanded an army of quotations, these invariably deserted her at the critical moment, and the only phrase she retained—*Canst thou draw out leviathan with a hook*?—was one she had never yet found occasion to apply.

To-day she felt that even the complete mastery of the volume would hardly have insured her self-possession; for she thought it probable that, even if she *did*, in some miraculous way, remember an Allusion, it would be only to find that Osric Dane used a different volume (Mrs. Leveret was convinced that literary people always carried them), and would consequently not recognise her quotations.

Mrs. Leveret's sense of being adrift was intensified by the appearance of Mrs. Ballinger's drawing-room. To a careless eye its aspect was unchanged; but those acquainted with Mrs. Ballinger's way of arranging her books would instantly have detected the marks of recent perturbation. Mrs. Ballinger's province, as a member of the Lunch Club, was the Book of the Day. On that, whatever it was, from a novel to a treatise on experimental psychology, she was confidently, authoritatively "up." What became of last year's books, or last week's even; what she did with the "subjects" she had previously professed with equal authority; no one had ever yet discovered. 'Her mind was an hotel where facts came and went like transient lodgers, without leaving their address behind, and frequently without paying for their board. It was Mrs. Ballinger's boast that she was "abreast with the Thought of the Day," and her pride that this advanced position should be expressed by the books on her table. These volumes, frequently renewed, and almost always damp from the press, bore names generally unfamiliar to Mrs. Leveret, and giving her, as she furtively scanned them, a disheartening glimpse of new fields of knowledge to be breathlessly traversed in Mrs. Ballinger's wake. But to-day a number of maturer-looking volumes were adroitly mingled with the *primeurs* of the press—Karl Marx jostled Professor Bergson, and the "Confessions of

St. Augustine" lay beside the last work on "Mendelism"; so that even to Mrs. Leveret's fluttered perceptions it was clear that Mrs. Ballinger didn't in the least know what Osric Dane was likely to talk about, and had taken measures to be prepared for anything. Mrs. Leveret felt like a passenger on an ocean steamer who is told that there is no immediate danger, but that she had better put on her life-belt.

It was a relief to be roused from these forebodings by Miss Van Vluyck's arrival.

"Well, my dear," the new-comer briskly asked her hostess, "what subjects are we to discuss to-day?"

Mrs. Ballinger was furtively replacing a volume of Wordsworth by a copy of Verlaine. "I hardly know," she said, somewhat nervously. "Perhaps we had better leave that to circumstances."

"Circumstances?" said Miss Van Vluyck drily. "That means, I suppose, that Laura Glyde will take the floor as usual, and we shall be deluged with literature."

Philanthropy and statistics were Miss Van Vluyck's province, and she resented any tendency to divert their guest's attention from these topics.

Mrs. Plinth at this moment appeared.

"Literature?" she protested in a tone of remonstrance. "But this is perfectly unexpected. I understood we were to talk of Osric Dane's novel."

Mrs. Ballinger winced at the discrimination, but let it pass. "We can hardly make that our chief subject—at least not *too* intentionally," she suggested. "Of course we can let our talk *drift* in that direction; but we ought to have some other topic as an introduction, and that is what I wanted to consult you about. The fact is, we know so little of Osric Dane's tastes and interests that it is difficult to make any special preparation."

"It may be difficult," said Mrs. Plinth with decision, "but it is necessary. I know what that happy-go-lucky principle leads to. As I told one of my nieces the other day, there are certain emergencies for which a lady should always be prepared. It's in shocking taste to wear colours when one pays a visit of condolence, or a last year's dress when there are reports that one's husband is on the wrong side of the market; and so it is with conversation. All I ask is that I should know beforehand what is to be talked about; then I feel sure of being able to say the proper thing."

"I quite agree with you," Mrs. Ballinger assented; "but—"

And at that instant, heralded by the fluttered parlourmaid, Osric Dane appeared upon the threshold.

Mrs. Leveret told her sister afterward that she had known at a glance what was coming. She saw that Osric Dane was not going to meet them half way. That distinguished personage had indeed entered with an air of compulsion not calculated to promote the easy exercise of hospitality. She looked as though she were about to be photographed for a new edition of her books.

"DEVOTION TO THE TRUTH IS THE HALLMARK OF MORALITY; THERE IS NO GREATER, NOBLER, MORE HEROIC FORM OF DEVOTION."

— AYN RAND

The desire to propitiate a divinity is generally in inverse ratio to its responsiveness, and the sense of discouragement produced by Osric Dane's entrance visibly increased the Lunch Club's eagerness to please her. Any lingering idea that she might consider herself under an obligation to her entertainers was at once dispelled by her manner: as Mrs. Leveret said afterward to her sister, she had a way of looking at you that made you feel as if there was something wrong with your hat. This evidence of greatness produced such an immediate impression on the ladies that a shudder of awe ran through them when Mrs. Roby, as their hostess led the great personage into the dining-room, turned back to whisper to the others: "What a brute she is!"

The hour about the table did not tend to revise this verdict. It was passed by Osric Dane in the silent deglutition of Mrs. Bollinger's menu, and by the members of the club in the emission of tentative platitudes which their guest seemed to swallow as perfunctorily as the successive courses of the luncheon.

Mrs. Ballinger's reluctance to fix a topic had thrown the club into a mental disarray which increased with the return to the drawing-room, where the actual business of discussion was to open. Each lady waited for the other to speak; and there was a general shock of disappointment when their hostess opened the conversation by the painfully commonplace enquiry. "Is this your first visit to Hillbridge?"

Even Mrs. Leveret was conscious that this was a bad beginning; and a vague impulse of deprecation made Miss Glyde interject: "It is a very small place indeed."

Mrs. Plinth bristled. "We have a great many representative people," she said, in the tone of one who speaks for her order.

Osric Dane turned to her. "What do they represent?" she asked.

Mrs. Plinth's constitutional dislike to being questioned was intensified by her sense of unpreparedness; and her reproachful glance passed the question on to Mrs. Ballinger.

"Why," said that lady, glancing in turn at the other members, "as a community I hope it is not too much to say that we stand for culture."

"For art—" Miss Glyde interjected.

"For art and literature," Mrs. Ballinger emended.

"And for sociology, I trust," snapped Miss Van Vluyck.

"We have a standard," said Mrs. Plinth, feeling herself suddenly secure on the vast expanse of a generalisation; and Mrs. Leveret, thinking there must be room for more than one on so broad a statement, took courage to murmur: "Oh, certainly; we have a standard."

"The object of our little club," Mrs. Ballinger continued, "is to concentrate the highest tendencies of Hillbridge—to centralise and focus its intellectual effort."

This was felt to be so happy that the ladies drew an almost audible breath of relief.

"We aspire," the President went on, "to be in touch with whatever is highest in art, literature and ethics."

Osric Dane again turned to her. "What ethics?" she asked.

A tremor of apprehension encircled the room. None of the ladies required any preparation to pronounce on a question of morals; but when they were called ethics it was different. The club, when fresh from the

"Encyclopaedia Britannica," the "Reader's Handbook" or Smith's "Classical Dictionary," could deal confidently with any subject; but when taken unawares it had been known to define agnosticism as a heresy of the Early Church and Professor Froude as a distinguished histologist; and such minor members as Mrs. Leveret still secretly regarded ethics as something vaguely pagan.

Even to Mrs. Ballinger, Osric Dane's question was unsettling, and there was a general sense of gratitude when Laura Glyde leaned forward to say, with her most sympathetic accent: "You must excuse us, Mrs. Dane, for not being able, just at present, to talk of anything but 'The Wings of Death.'"

"Yes," said Miss Van Vluyck, with a sudden resolve to carry the war into the enemy's camp. "We are so anxious to know the exact purpose you had in mind in writing your wonderful book."

"You will find," Mrs. Plinth interposed, "that we are not superficial readers."

"We are eager to hear from you," Miss Van Vluyck continued, "if the pessimistic tendency of the book is an expression of your own convictions or—"

"Or merely," Miss Glyde thrust in, "a sombre background brushed in to throw your figures into more vivid relief. *Are* you not primarily plastic?"

"I have always maintained," Mrs. Ballinger interposed, "that you represent the purely objective method—"

Osric Dane helped herself critically to coffee. "How do you define objective?" she then enquired.

There was a flurried pause before Laura Glyde intensely murmured: "In reading *you* we don't define, we feel."

Otsric Dane smiled. "The cerebellum," she remarked, "is not infrequently the seat of the literary emotions." And she took a second lump of sugar.

The sting that this remark was vaguely felt to conceal was almost neutralised by the satisfaction of being addressed in such technical language.

"Ah, the cerebellum," said Miss Van Vluyck complacently. "The club took a course in psychology last winter."

"Which psychology?" asked Osric Dane.

There was an agonising pause, during which each member of the club secretly deplored the distressing inefficiency of the others. Only Mrs. Roby went on placidly sipping her chartreuse. At last Mrs. Ballinger said, with an attempt at a high tone: "Well, really, you know, it was last year that we took psychology, and this winter we have been so absorbed in—"

She broke off, nervously trying to recall some of the club's discussions; but her faculties seemed to be paralysed by the petrifying stare of Osric Dane. What *had* the club been absorbed in? Mrs. Ballinger, with a vague purpose of gaining time, repeated slowly: "We've been so intensely absorbed in—"

Mrs. Roby put down her liqueur glass and drew near the group with a smile.

"In Xingu?" she gently prompted.

A thrill ran through the other members. They exchanged confused glances, and then, with one accord, turned a gaze of mingled relief and interrogation on their rescuer. The expression of each denoted a different phase of the same emotion. Mrs. Plinth was the first to compose her features to an air of reassurance: after a moment's hasty adjustment her look almost implied that it was she who had given the word to Mrs. Ballinger.

"Xingu, of course!" exclaimed the latter with her accustomed promptness, while Miss Van Vluyck and Laura Glyde seemed to be plumbing the depths of memory, and Mrs. Leveret, feeling apprehensively for Appropriate Allusions, was somehow reassured by the uncomfortable pressure of its bulk against her person.

"ALL ART DEALS WITH THE ABSURD AND AIMS AT THE SIMPLE. GOOD ART SPEAKS TRUTH, INDEED IS TRUTH, PERHAPS THE ONLY TRUTH."
— IRIS MURDOCH

Osric Dane's change of countenance was no less striking than that of her entertainers. She too put down her coffee-cup, but with a look of distinct annoyance; she too wore, for a brief moment, what Mrs. Roby afterward described as the look of feeling for something in the back of her head; and before she could dissemble these momentary signs of weakness, Mrs. Roby, turning to her with a deferential smile, had said: "And we've been so hoping that to-day you would tell us just what you think of it."

Osric Dane received the homage of the smile as a matter of course; but the accompanying question obviously embarrassed her, and it became clear to her observers that she was not quick at shifting her facial scenery. It was as though her countenance had so long been set in an expression of unchallenged superiority that the muscles had stiffened, and refused to obey her orders.

"Xingu—" she said, as if seeking in her turn to gain time.

Mrs. Roby continued to press her. "Knowing how engrossing the subject is, you will understand how it happens that the club has let everything else go to the wall for the moment. Since we took up Xingu I might almost say—were it not for your books—that nothing else seems to us worth remembering."

Osric Dane's stern features were darkened rather than lit up by an uneasy smile. "I am glad to hear that you make one exception," she gave out between narrowed lips.

"Oh, of course," Mrs. Roby said prettily; "but as you have shown us that—so very naturally!—you don't care to talk of your own things, we really can't let you off from telling us exactly what you think about Xingu; especially," she added, with a still more persuasive smile, "as some people say that one of your last books was saturated with it."

It was an *it*, then—the assurance sped like fire through the parched minds of the other members. In their eagerness to gain the least little clue to Xingu they almost forgot the joy of assisting at the discomfiture of Mrs. Dane.

The latter reddened nervously under her antagonist's challenge. "May I ask," she faltered out, "to which of my books you refer?"

Mrs. Roby did not falter. "That's just what I want you to tell us; because, though I was present, I didn't actually take part."

"Present at what?" Mrs. Dane took her up; and for an instant the trembling members of the Lunch Club thought that the champion Providence had raised up for them had lost a point. But Mrs. Roby explained herself gaily: "At the discussion, of course. And so we're dreadfully anxious to know just how it was that you went into the Xingu."

There was a portentous pause, a silence so big with incalculable dangers that the members with one accord checked the words on their lips, like soldiers dropping their arms to watch a single combat between their leaders. Then Mrs. Dane gave expression to their inmost dread by saying sharply: "Ah—you say *the* Xingu, do you?"

Mrs. Roby smiled undauntedly. "It is a shade pedantic, isn't it? Personally, I always drop the article; but I don't know how the other members feel about it."

The other members looked as though they would willingly have dispensed with this appeal to their opinion, and Mrs. Roby, after a bright glance about the group, went on: "They probably think, as I do, that nothing really matters except the thing itself—except Xingu."

No immediate reply seemed to occur to Mrs. Dane, and Mrs. Ballinger gathered courage to say: "Surely every one must feel that about Xingu."

Mrs. Plinth came to her support with a heavy murmur of assent, and Laura Glyde sighed out emotionally: "I have known cases where it has changed a whole life."

"It has done me worlds of good," Mrs. Leveret interjected, seeming to herself to remember that she had either taken it or read it the winter before.

"Of course," Mrs. Roby admitted, "the difficulty is that one must give up so much time to it. It's very long."

"I can't imagine," said Miss Van Vluyck, "grudging the time given to such a subject."

"And deep in places," Mrs. Roby pursued; (so then it was a book!) "And it isn't easy to skip."

"I never skip," said Mrs. Plinth dogmatically.

"Ah, it's dangerous to, in Xingu. Even at the start there are places where one can't. One must just wade through."

"I should hardly call it *wading*," said Mrs. Ballinger sarcastically.

Mrs. Roby sent her a look of interest. "Ah—you always found it went swimmingly?"

Mrs. Ballinger hesitated. "Of course there are difficult passages," she conceded.

"Yes; some are not at all clear—even," Mrs. Roby added, "if one is familiar with the original."

"As I suppose you are?" Osric Dane interposed, suddenly fixing her with a look of challenge.

Mrs. Roby met it by a deprecating gesture. "Oh, it's really not difficult up to a certain point; though some of the branches are very little known, and it's almost impossible to get at the source."

"Have you ever tried?" Mrs. Plinth enquired, still distrustful of Mrs. Roby's thoroughness.

"THE NOBILITY OF OUR CRAFT WILL ALWAYS BE ROOTED IN TWO COMMITMENTS, DIFFICULT TO MAINTAIN: THE REFUSAL TO LIE ABOUT WHAT ONE KNOWS AND THE RESISTANCE TO OPPRESSION."

— ALBERT CAMUS

Mrs. Roby was silent for a moment; then she replied with lowered lids: "No—but a friend of mine did; a very brilliant man; and he told me it was best for women—not to...."

A shudder ran around the room. Mrs. Leveret coughed so that the parlour-maid, who was handing the cigarettes, should not hear; Miss Van Vluyck's face took on a nauseated expression, and Mrs. Plinth looked as if she were passing some one she did not care to bow to. But the most remarkable result of Mrs. Roby's words was the effect they produced on the Lunch Club's distinguished guest. Osric Dane's impassive features suddenly softened to an expression of the warmest human sympathy, and edging her chair toward Mrs. Roby's she asked: "Did he really? And—did you find he was right?"

Mrs. Ballinger, in whom annoyance at Mrs. Roby's unwonted assumption of prominence was beginning to displace gratitude for the aid she had rendered, could not consent to her being allowed, by such dubious means, to monopolise the attention of their guest. If Osric Dane had not enough self-respect to resent Mrs. Roby's flippancy, at least the Lunch Club would do so in the person of its President.

Mrs. Ballinger laid her hand on Mrs. Roby's arm. "We must not forget," she said with a frigid amiability, "that absorbing as Xingu is to *us*, it may be less interesting to—"

"Oh, no, on the contrary, I assure you," Osric Dane intervened.

"—to others," Mrs. Ballinger finished firmly; "and we must not allow our little meeting to end without persuading Mrs. Dane to say a few words to us on a subject which, to-day, is much more present in all our thoughts. I refer, of course, to 'The Wings of Death.'"

The other members, animated by various degrees of the same sentiment, and encouraged by the humanised mien of their redoubtable guest, repeated after Mrs. Ballinger: "Oh, yes, you really *must* talk to us a little about your book."

Osric Dane's expression became as bored, though not as haughty, as when her work had been previously mentioned. But before she could respond to Mrs. Ballinger's request, Mrs. Roby had risen from her seat, and was pulling down her veil over her frivolous nose.

"I'm so sorry," she said, advancing toward her hostess with outstretched hand, "but before Mrs. Dane begins I think I'd better run away. Unluckily, as you know, I haven't read her books, so I should be at a terrible disadvantage among you all, and besides, I've an engagement to play bridge."

If Mrs. Roby had simply pleaded her ignorance of Osric Dane's works as a reason for withdrawing, the Lunch Club, in view of her recent prowess, might have approved such evidence of discretion; but to couple this excuse with the brazen announcement that she was foregoing the privilege for the purpose of joining a bridge-party was only one more instance of her deplorable lack of discrimination.

The ladies were disposed, however, to feel that her departure—now that she had performed the sole service she was ever likely to render them—would probably make for greater order and dignity in the impending discussion, besides relieving them of the sense of self-distrust which her presence always mysteriously produced. Mrs. Ballinger therefore restricted herself to a formal murmur of regret, and the other members were just grouping themselves comfortably about Osric Dane when the latter, to their dismay, started up from the sofa on which she had been seated.

"Oh wait—do wait, and I'll go with you!" she called out to Mrs. Roby; and, seizing the hands of the disconcerted members, she administered a series of farewell pressures with the mechanical haste of a railway-conductor punching tickets.

"I'm so sorry—I'd quite forgotten—" she flung back at them from the threshold; and as she joined Mrs. Roby, who had turned in surprise at her appeal, the other ladies had the mortification of hearing her say, in a voice which she did not take the pains to lower: "If you'll let me walk a little way with you, I should so like to ask you a few more questions about Xingu...."

III

The incident had been so rapid that the door closed on the departing pair before the other members had time to understand what was happening. Then a sense of the indignity put upon them by Osric Dane's unceremonious desertion began to contend with the confused feeling that they had been cheated out of their due without exactly knowing how or why.

There was a silence, during which Mrs. Ballinger, with a perfunctory hand, rearranged the skilfully grouped literature at which her distinguished guest had not so much as glanced; then Miss Van Vluyck tartly pronounced: "Well, I can't say that I consider Osric Dane's departure a great loss."

This confession crystallised the resentment of the other members, and Mrs. Leveret exclaimed: "I do believe she came on purpose to be nasty!"

It was Mrs. Plinth's private opinion that Osric Dane's attitude toward the Lunch Club might have been very different had it welcomed her in the majestic setting of the Plinth drawing-rooms; but not liking to reflect on the inadequacy of Mrs. Ballinger's establishment she sought a roundabout satisfaction in depreciating her lack of foresight.

"I said from the first that we ought to have had a subject ready. It's what always happens when you're unprepared. Now if we'd only got up Xingu—"

The slowness of Mrs. Plinth's mental processes was always allowed for by the club; but this instance of it was too much for Mrs. Ballinger's equanimity.

"Xingu!" she scoffed. "Why, it was the fact of our knowing so much more about it than she did—unprepared though we were—that made Osric Dane so furious. I should have thought that was plain enough to everybody!"

This retort impressed even Mrs. Plinth, and Laura Glyde, moved by an impulse of generosity, said: "Yes, we really ought to be grateful to Mrs. Roby for introducing the topic. It may have made Osric Dane furious, but at least it made her civil."

"I am glad we were able to show her," added Miss Van Vluyck, "that a broad and up-to-date culture is not confined to the great intellectual centres."

This increased the satisfaction of the other members, and they began to forget their wrath against Osric Dane in the pleasure of having contributed to her discomfiture.

Miss Van Vluyck thoughtfully rubbed her spectacles. "What surprised me most," she continued, "was that Fanny Roby should be so up on Xingu."

This remark threw a slight chill on the company, but Mrs. Ballinger said with an air of indulgent irony: "Mrs. Roby always has the knack of making a little go a long way; still, we certainly owe her a debt for happening to remember that she'd heard of Xingu." And this was felt by the other members to be a graceful way of cancelling once for all the club's obligation to Mrs. Roby.

"NOTHING IS LESS REAL THAN REALISM. DETAILS ARE CONFUSING. IT IS ONLY BY SELECTION, BY ELIMINATION, BY EMPHASIS, THAT WE GET AT THE REAL MEANING OF THINGS."
— GEORGIA O'KEEFFE

Even Mrs. Leveret took courage to speed a timid shaft of irony. "I fancy Osric Dane hardly expected to take a lesson in Xingu at Hillbridge!"

Mrs. Ballinger smiled. "When she asked me what we represented—do you remember?—I wish I'd simply said we represented Xingu!"

All the ladies laughed appreciatively at this sally, except Mrs. Plinth, who said, after a moment's deliberation: "I'm not sure it would have been wise to do so."

Mrs. Ballinger, who was already beginning to feel as if she had launched at Osric Dane the retort which had just occurred to her, turned ironically on Mrs. Plinth. "May I ask why?" she enquired.

Mrs. Plinth looked grave. "Surely," she said, "I understood from Mrs. Roby herself that the subject was one it was as well not to go into too deeply?"

Miss Van Vluyck rejoined with precision: "I think that applied only to an investigation of the origin of the—of the—"; and suddenly she found that her usually accurate memory had failed her. "It's a part of the subject I never studied myself/," she concluded.

"Nor I," said Mrs. Ballinger.

Laura Glyde bent toward them with widened eyes. "And yet it seems—doesn't it?—the part that is fullest of an esoteric fascination?"

"I don't know on what you base that," said Miss Van Vluyck argumentatively.

"Well, didn't you notice how intensely interested Osric Dane became as soon as she heard what the brilliant foreigner—he *was* a foreigner, wasn't he?—had told Mrs. Roby about the origin—the origin of the rite—or whatever you call it?"

Mrs. Plinth looked disapproving, and Mrs. Ballinger visibly wavered. Then she said: "It may not be desirable to touch on the—on that part of the subject in general conversation; but, from the importance it evidently has to a woman of Osric Dane's distinction, I feel as if we ought not to be afraid to discuss it among ourselves—without gloves—though with closed doors, if necessary."

"I'm quite of your opinion," Miss Van Vluyck came briskly to her support; "on condition, that is, that all grossness of language is avoided."

"Oh, I'm sure we shall understand without that," Mrs. Leveret tittered; and Laura Glyde added significantly: "I fancy we can read between the lines," while Mrs. Ballinger rose to assure herself that the doors were really closed.

Mrs. Plinth had not yet given her adhesion. "I hardly see," she began, "what benefit is to be derived from investigating such peculiar customs—"

But Mrs. Ballinger's patience had reached the extreme limit of tension. "This at least," she returned; "that we shall not be placed again in the humiliating position of finding ourselves less up on our own subjects than Fanny Roby!"

Even to Mrs. Plinth this argument was conclusive. She peered furtively about the room and lowered her commanding tones to ask: "Have you got a copy?"

"A—a copy?" stammered Mrs. Ballinger. She was aware that the other members were looking at her expectantly, and that this answer was inadequate, so she supported it by asking another question. "A copy of what?"

Her companions bent their expectant gaze on Mrs. Plinth, who, in turn, appeared less sure of herself than usual. "Why, of—of—the book," she explained.

"What book?" snapped Miss Van Vluyck, almost as sharply as Osric Dane.

Mrs. Ballinger looked at Laura Glyde, whose eyes were interrogatively fixed on Mrs. Leveret. The fact of being deferred to was so new to the latter that it filled her with an insane temerity. "Why, Xingu, of course!" she exclaimed.

A profound silence followed this challenge to the resources of Mrs. Ballinger's library, and the latter, after glancing nervously toward the Books of the Day, returned with dignity: "It's not a thing one cares to leave about."

"I should think not!" exclaimed Mrs. Plinth.

"It *is* a book, then?" said Miss Van Vluyck.

This again threw the company into disarray, and Mrs. Ballinger, with an impatient sigh, rejoined: "Why—there *is* a book—naturally...."

"Then why did Miss Glyde call it a religion?"

Laura Glyde started up. "A religion? I never—"

"Yes, you did," Miss Van Vluyck insisted; "you spoke of rites; and Mrs. Plinth said it was a custom."

Miss Glyde was evidently making a desperate effort to recall her statement; but accuracy of detail was not her strongest point. At length she began in a deep murmur: "Surely they used to do something of the kind at the Eleusinian mysteries—"

"Oh—" said Miss Van Vluyck, on the verge of disapproval; and Mrs. Plinth protested: "I understood there was to be no indelicacy!"

Mrs. Ballinger could not control her irritation. "Really, it is too bad that we should not be able to talk the matter over quietly among ourselves. Personally, I think that if one goes into Xingu at all—"

"Oh, so do I!" cried Miss Glyde.

"And I don't see how one can avoid doing so, if one wishes to keep up with the Thought of the Day—"

Mrs. Leveret uttered an exclamation of relief. "There—that's it!" she interposed.

"IF YOU DO NOT TELL THE TRUTH ABOUT YOURSELF YOU CANNOT TELL IT ABOUT OTHER PEOPLE."
— VIRGINIA WOOLF

"What's it?" the President took her up.

"Why—it's a—a Thought: I mean a philosophy."

This seemed to bring a certain relief to Mrs. Ballinger and Laura Glyde, but Miss Van Vluyck said: "Excuse me if I tell you that you're all mistaken. Xingu happens to be a language."

"A language!" the Lunch Club cried.

"Certainly. Don't you remember Fanny Roby's saying that there were several branches, and that some were hard to trace? What could that apply to but dialects?"

Mrs. Ballinger could no longer restrain a contemptuous laugh. "Really, if the Lunch Club has reached such a pass that it has to go to Fanny Roby for instruction on a subject like Xingu, it had almost better cease to exist!"

"It's really her fault for not being clearer," Laura Glyde put in.

"Oh, clearness and Fanny Roby!" Mrs. Ballinger shrugged. "I daresay we shall find she was mistaken on almost every point."

"Why not look it up?" said Mrs. Plinth.

As a rule this recurrent suggestion of Mrs. Plinth's was ignored in the heat of discussion, and only resorted to afterward in the privacy of each member's home. But on the present occasion the desire to ascribe their own confusion of thought to the vague and contradictory nature of Mrs. Roby's statements caused the members of the Lunch Club to utter a collective demand for a book of reference.

At this point the production of her treasured volume gave Mrs. Leveret, for a moment, the unusual experience of occupying the centre front; but she was not able to hold it long, for Appropriate Allusions contained no mention of Xingu.

"Oh, that's not the kind of thing we want!" exclaimed Miss Van Vluyck. She cast a disparaging glance over Mrs. Ballinger's assortment of literature, and added impatiently: "Haven't you any useful books?"

"Of course I have," replied Mrs. Ballinger indignantly; "I keep them in my husband's dressing-room."

From this region, after some difficulty and delay, the parlour-maid produced the W-Z volume of an Encyclopaedia and, in deference to the fact that the demand for it had come from Miss Van Vluyck, laid the ponderous tome before her.

There was a moment of painful suspense while Miss Van Vluyck rubbed her spectacles, adjusted them, and turned to Z; and a murmur of surprise when she said: "It isn't here."

"I suppose," said Mrs. Plinth, "it's not fit to be put in a book of reference."

"Oh, nonsense!" exclaimed Mrs. Ballinger. "Try X."

Miss Van Vluyck turned back through the volume, peering short-sightedly up and down the pages, till she came to a stop and remained motionless, like a dog on a point.

"Well, have you found it?" Mrs. Ballinger enquired after a considerable delay.

"Yes. I've found it," said Miss Van Vluyck in a queer voice.

Mrs. Plinth hastily interposed: "I beg you

won't read it aloud if there's anything offensive."

Miss Van Vluyck, without answering, continued her silent scrutiny.

"Well, what *is* it?" exclaimed Laura Glyde excitedly.

"*Do* tell us!" urged Mrs. Leveret, feeling that she would have something awful to tell her sister.

Miss Van Vluyck pushed the volume aside and turned slowly toward the expectant group.

"It's a river."

"A *river?*"

"Yes: in Brazil. Isn't that where she's been living?"

"Who? Fanny Roby? Oh, but you must be mistaken. You've been reading the wrong thing," Mrs. Ballinger exclaimed, leaning over her to seize the volume.

"It's the only Xingu in the Encyclopaedia; and she *has* been living in Brazil," Miss Van Vluyck persisted.

"Yes: her brother has a consulship there," Mrs. Leveret interposed.

"But it's too ridiculous! I—we—why we *all* remember studying Xingu last year—or the year before last," Mrs. Ballinger stammered.

"I thought I did when *you* said so," Laura Glyde avowed.

"I said so?" cried Mrs. Ballinger.

"Yes. You said it had crowded everything else out of your mind."

"Well *you* said it had changed your whole life!"

"For that matter. Miss Van Vluyck said she had never grudged the time she'd given it."

Mrs. Plinth interposed: "I made it clear that I knew nothing whatever of the original."

Mrs. Ballinger broke off the dispute with a groan. "Oh, what does it all matter if she's been making fools of us? I believe Miss Van Vluyck's right—she was talking of the river all the while!"

"How could she? It's too preposterous," Miss Glyde exclaimed.

"Listen." Miss Van Vluyck had repossessed herself of the Encyclopaedia, and restored her spectacles to a nose reddened by excitement.

"STORYTELLING REVEALS MEANING WITHOUT COMMITTING THE ERROR OF DEFINING IT."

— HANNAH ARENDT

"'The Xingu, one of the principal rivers of Brazil, rises on the plateau of Mato Grosso, and flows in a northerly direction for a length of no less than one thousand one hundred and eighteen miles, entering the Amazon near the mouth of the latter river. The upper course of the Xingu is auriferous and fed by numerous branches. Its source was first discovered in 1884 by the German explorer von den Steinen, after a difficult and dangerous expedition through a region inhabited by tribes still in the Stone Age of culture.'"

The ladies received this communication in a state of stupefied silence from which Mrs. Leveret was the first to rally. "She certainly *did* speak of its having branches."

The word seemed to snap the last thread of their incredulity. "And of its great length," gasped Mrs. Ballinger.

"She said it was awfully deep, and you couldn't skip—you just had to wade through," Miss Glyde added.

The idea worked its way more slowly through Mrs. Plinth's compact resistances. "How could there be anything improper about a river?" she enquired.

"Improper?"

"Why, what she said about the source—that it was corrupt?"

"Not corrupt, but hard to get at," Laura Glyde corrected. "Some one who'd been there had told her so. I daresay it was the explorer himself—doesn't it say the expedition was dangerous?"

"'Difficult and dangerous,'" read Miss Van Vluyck.

Mrs. Ballinger pressed her hands to her throbbing temples. "There's nothing she said that wouldn't apply to a river—to this river!" She swung about excitedly to the other members. "Why, do you remember her telling us that she hadn't read 'The Supreme Instant' because she'd taken it on a boating party while she was staying with her brother, and some one had 'shied' it overboard—'shied' of course was her own expression."

The ladies breathlessly signified that the expression had not escaped them.

"Well—and then didn't she tell Osric Dane that one of her books was simply saturated with Xingu? Of course it was, if one of Mrs. Roby's rowdy friends had thrown it into the river!"

This surprising reconstruction of the scene in which they had just participated left the members of the Lunch Club inarticulate. At length, Mrs. Plinth, after visibly labouring with the problem, said in a heavy tone: "Osric Dane was taken in too."

Mrs. Leveret took courage at this. "Perhaps that's what Mrs. Roby did it for. She said Osric Dane was a brute, and she may have wanted to give her a lesson."

Miss Van Vluyck frowned. "It was hardly worth while to do it at our expense."

"At least," said Miss Glyde with a touch of bitterness, "she succeeded in interesting her, which was more than we did."

"What chance had we?" rejoined Mrs. Ballinger.

"Mrs. Roby monopolised her from the first. And *that*, I've no doubt, was her purpose—to give Osric Dane a false impression of her own standing in the club. She would hesitate at nothing to attract attention: we all know how she took in poor Professor Foreland."

"She actually makes him give bridge-teas every Thursday," Mrs. Leveret piped up.

Laura Glyde struck her hands together. "Why, this is Thursday, and it's *there* she's gone, of course; and taken Osric with her!"

"And they're shrieking over us at this moment," said Mrs. Ballinger between her teeth.

This possibility seemed too preposterous to be admitted. "She would hardly dare," said Miss Van Vluyck, "confess the imposture to Osric Dane."

"I'm not so sure: I thought I saw her make a sign as she left. If she hadn't made a sign, why should Osric Dane have rushed out after her?"

"Well, you know, we'd all been telling her how wonderful Xingu was, and she said she wanted to find out more about it," Mrs. Leveret said, with a tardy impulse of justice to the absent.

This reminder, far from mitigating the wrath of the other members, gave it a stronger impetus.

"Yes—and that's exactly what they're both laughing over now," said Laura Glyde ironically.

Mrs. Plinth stood up and gathered her expensive furs about her monumental form. "I have no wish to criticise," she said; "but unless the Lunch Club can protect its members against the recurrence of such—such unbecoming scenes, I for one—"

"Oh, so do I!" agreed Miss Glyde, rising also.

Miss Van Vluyck closed the Encyclopaedia and proceeded to button herself into her jacket "My time is really too valuable—" she began.

"I fancy we are all of one mind," said Mrs. Ballinger, looking searchingly at Mrs. Leveret, who looked at the others.

"I always deprecate anything like a scandal—" Mrs. Plinth continued.

"She has been the cause of one to-day!" exclaimed Miss Glyde.

Mrs. Leveret moaned: "I don't see how she *could!*" and Miss Van Vluyck said, picking up her note-book: "Some women stop at nothing."

"—but if," Mrs. Plinth took up her argument impressively, "anything of the kind had happened in *my* house" (it never would have, her tone implied), "I should have felt that I owed it to myself either to ask for Mrs. Roby's resignation—or to offer mine."

"ONE WORD OF TRUTH SHALL OUTWEIGH THE WHOLE WORLD."
— ALEKSANDR SOLZHENITSYN

"Oh, Mrs. Plinth—" gasped the Lunch Club.

"Fortunately for me," Mrs. Plinth continued with an awful magnanimity, "the matter was taken out of my hands by our President's decision that the right to entertain distinguished guests was a privilege vested in her office; and I think the other members will agree that, as she was alone in this opinion, she ought to be alone in deciding on the best way of effacing its—its really deplorable consequences."

A deep silence followed this outbreak of Mrs. Plinth's long-stored resentment.

"I don't see why I should be expected to ask her to resign—" Mrs. Ballinger at length began; but Laura Glyde turned back to remind her: "You know she made you say that you'd got on swimmingly in Xingu."

An ill-timed giggle escaped from Mrs. Leveret, and Mrs. Ballinger energetically continued "—but you needn't think for a moment that I'm afraid to!"

The door of the drawing-room closed on the retreating backs of the Lunch Club, and the President of that distinguished association, seating herself at her writing-table, and pushing away a copy of "The Wings of Death" to make room for her elbow, drew forth a sheet of the club's note-paper, on which she began to write: "My dear Mrs. Roby—"

READERS FIRST

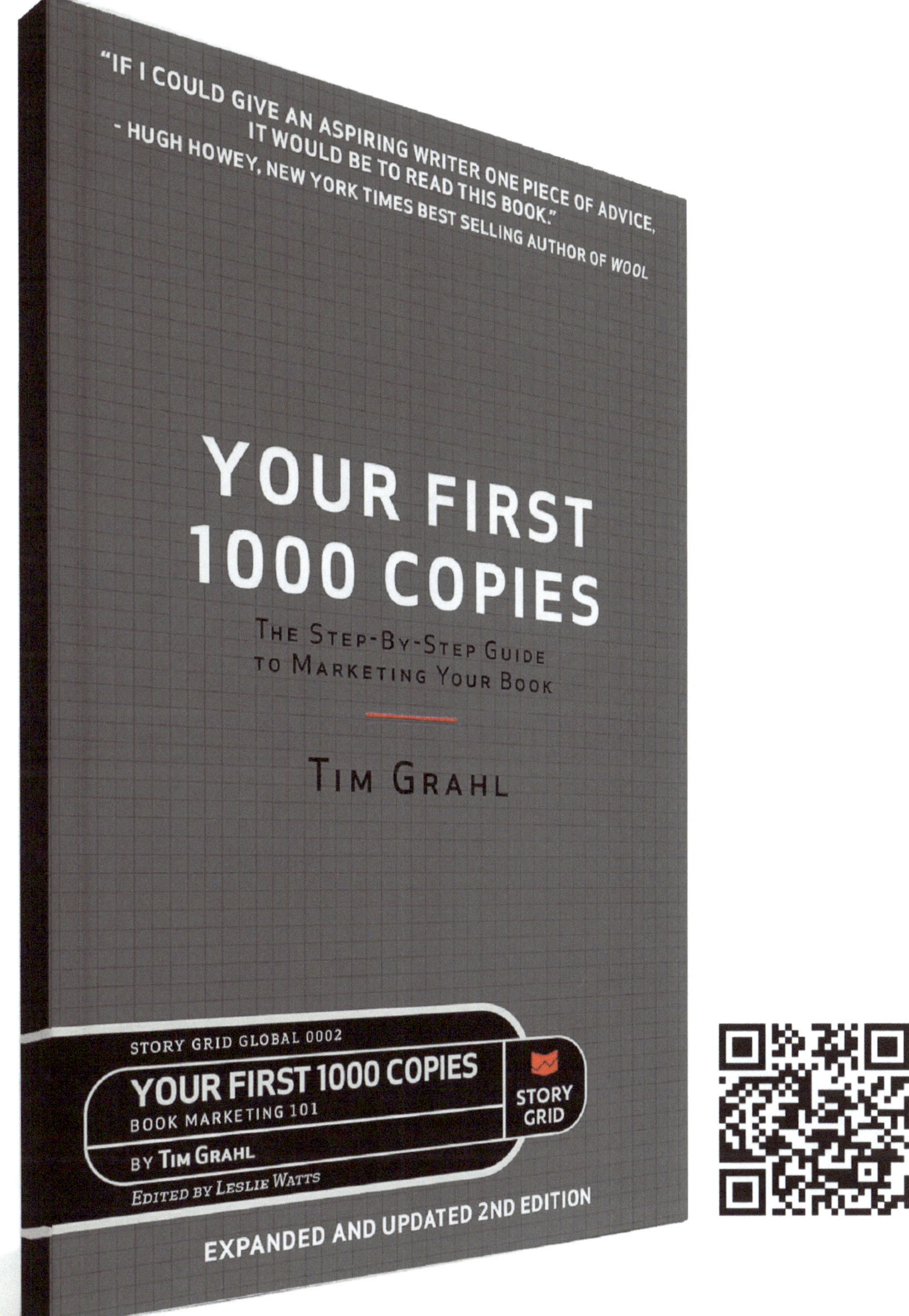

"Tim Grahl is fast becoming a legend, almost single-handedly changing the way authors around the world spread ideas and connect with readers."
— Daniel H. Pink, #1 *New York Times* bestselling author of *Drive*

THE LIVES WE DREAM AND DO NOT REALIZE

The Story Grid Mission Statement

SHAWN COYNE

PHOTOGRAPHY BY VICTOR CASTRO

Edited by Tim Grahl

"Pray for the dead, fight like hell for the living." —Mary Harris "Mother" Jones, 1837–1930

The Boxer
New York, New York, September 19, 2024
4:59 a.m

In the penultimate minute of the darkest hour just before dawn, I found myself writing this:

If I were offered the following deal:

All of the assets I've created will be liquidated and allocated to my surviving wife so that our children:

1. *Will be able to finish college without having to take on debt and*
2. *Have some money left over to get them started in their lives, meaning they will have enough to be able to find gainful employment or start a small business and someday afford to buy a house and start a family of their own*

In exchange for:

My life...

At this moment, I would make that trade.

Rereading those sad words, I now sit wondering why I felt that way.

I take comfort in the probability that Arthur Miller must have felt similarly when he wrote *Death of a Salesman*, which presaged the even more tragic and absurd *The Crucible*. We both fell into a disturbing liminality, regardless of how we got there.

I realize my confession is about wanting to return to wherever I came from. If I were Sigmund Freud, I'd call it that death wish as a resisting of the demands of the future. But it's paradoxically bound to another need.

This is the need to carry on, persisting against the past, as represented by my desire to leave a sustaining legacy for my family. And just like Willy Loman and no doubt his creator, Arthur Miller, late at night, my remembrances of past travails and projections of future tribulations swirl within. I grow ever wearier of the incessant internal jabbering.

Will it never cease?

The inner war is the assault of would haves, could haves, and should haves—a simultaneous longing for those painful internal tormenting fires to burn out but a knowing that their secession would be an abandonment of our purposeful calling within. So, like pugilists at rest, we look toward the heavens and steel ourselves for another round with our internal and external foes.

A bronze statue, a Hellenistic Greek original circa 330 to 50 BCE, of unknown origin resides at Palazzo Massimo alle Terme. It depicts an ancient boxer in between bouts. It is known as an example of the movement away from idealized depictions of the body and toward emotional and psychological realism.

What does it mean when a society defines a person as worth more dead than alive? That's absurd. Isn't it?

There must be other kinds of legacies than simply the objective quantitative means of purchasing stuff to pass on to one's heirs.

What of those legacies?

The warm feelings, thoughtful care, and demonstrative expressions of wanting what's best for others?

Shouldn't those legacies be celebrated and passed on with more vigor and emphasis than indexical bank liquidations and asset transfers?

Obviously, yes.

The loss my family would have to confront upon my sudden physical absence would be catastrophic. No amount of money could or would assuage it. I'm certainly more than the sum of my purchasing power.

It occurs to me now that those dark thoughts were not really indicative of my desire to quit. Instead, they were about changing course, getting back in the ring to become something and someone different from who I am now. The dark depths opened up for me as the means to realize I've hit a crossroads, that there is more to me and my work than just the fruits of the labor and the contemplation of its justification.

Far more.

And it's a weird crossroad because it's not about me anymore.

It's about **you.**

II

Ten Years Gone
New York, New York, September 19, 2014
11:54 p.m

I'm alone in a windowless back room of an office building on New York's Vandam Street, just north of the Holland Tunnel, when I upload my first blog post to www.storygrid.com.

I built the website by myself, from scratch.

I resolved to do so after reading a book. I'd just turned fifty years old, and the old dog was curious about these new tricks. After finding the book compelling, I enrolled in the author's online course to better understand the practicalities of communicating with strangers on the internet's brave, relatively new World Wide Web.

Lastly, I followed the step-by-step procedure he—a stranger who lived in Lynchburg, Virginia—instructed me to follow to effectively announce my grandiose intention to teach the world how to tell better stories with clarity and conviction.

I can't explain why *I*, a grizzled book publishing veteran with extensive marketing and publishing experience launching bestselling projects, put my faith in someone I'd never met. The inescapable truth was that I needed a mentor to help me best present my life's work directly to a not yet known—and very possibly marginal—audience. Turn and face the strange. What I can describe is a weird intuition that whoever this guy was, following him was my best bad choice.

The truth was, even at this late stage of life, I didn't know who I was. So, naturally, I was unsure of how to present whatever I thought I could be in this alien environment. Due to a series of spectacularly incendiary (innovative but risky) decisions over my then twenty-four-year publishing career, I now sat in the aforementioned small windowless fortress of solitude running a one-man literary agency.

I rented the converted closet from a colleague who'd taken pity on me. She'd continue to do so as long as I continued to hand over $1,235.00 a month. For New York real estate, it was more than a fair deal.

Inside my bubble, I made a nice, prosperous living; to characterize it otherwise would be facetious, but I knew I was squandering my potential. The money was fine, but I wanted more out of my fourteen-hour working days than that.

You see, I'd been lied to unintentionally (and intentionally) innumerable times about all manner of personal, professional, and existential matters by caring (and uncaring) people in the world I'd chosen to live in. Hence, my eventual barricading of myself on Vandam, metaphorically living alone, alienated in a book-publishing version of a *van down by the river.*

"His future is behind him," is how a former mentor would have described me back then. Ever the mercurial fighter of status quo authority, I set out to prove him wrong. Not that he or any other of my former colleagues were paying attention to my self-imposed exile. They had their own shit to contend with, and I was, in all likelihood, one of the furthest things from their minds. But as we all need projections of antagonism to spur us on, my tyrannical former boss fit the bill.

The core of my life's work had yet to be publicly presented. I had in mind the scientific construction of a narrative theory that was "not magical" but also "not formulaic," rather Platonic and formally derived from Aristotle's *Poetics*. The truth was that few in my coterie—the New York and International Literary Circles—were interested in it. Though few, if any, had read Aristotle, they thought it was an impossible quixotic dream. And in their estimation, encouraging such a pursuit would be ill-advised. Better to keep my head down and turn the best-seller crank as best I could like the rest of them.

When I began to explain my propositions, I was invariably met with dismissive variations of that old saw, "Everyone knows storytelling is subjective." It was as if they'd all received the same software program and would not critically investigate the factory settings' specious assumptions. I knew because I'd been programmed by the same one in my "higher education" training. What I'd been told about storytelling rang absolutely false to me. Why? Because of the axiomatic paradoxical assumption that it was both unscientific noncausal "subjective opinion," code words for meaninglessness, and historically causal of virtuous and perverse behavior, meaningful "good and bad narratives" —absurd.

This idealized refrain—which cryptically separates the population into those born with an innate ability to tell causal stories and those who weren't—is still one of the dominant misconceptions of our time. Most people cling to its veracity as strongly as nihilists cling to absurdity. Often, those nihilist/absurdist clingers are one and the same. They speak of "controlling the narrative," as only the innate storytellers, the "special, chosen ones among the ignorant hordes," can do. This notion goes back to Plato's *Republic* and his proposition that storytelling should be in the hands of philosopher kings, not persuasive propagandists. However, that's a can of worms best left for another investigation.

"The only way into truth is through one's own annihilation; through dwelling a long time in a state of extreme and total humiliation."

— Simone Weil

Storytelling is a scale-invariant universal. And all observers show and tell stories.

This historical and contemporary reality is inescapable—the misunderstanding of storytelling not as an integral scientific, spiritual, and philosophical practice but as a manipulative tool to use against the environment and the suckers who can't figure out who, how, or why they're being played. Its evidencing is so disturbing that it brings me to despair. Hence, my not-infrequent late-night musings about throwing in the proverbial towel and playing along with that mischaracterization for my own private fame and fortune. Why not just turn that bestseller crank and chuck the narrative theory stuff?

Thus, when at last deciding to "go public" with my propositions that meld the two intellectual cultures (Story is indicative of the humanities, and Grid is indicative of science), I thought it made sense to seek help elsewhere, far away from the maddening crowd of New York publishing. And culturally, you can't get further away from Manhattan than Lynchburg, Virginia.

But would anyone hear my call and respond to my www.storygrid.com channel? Who knew?

For decades, I'd read, written (as a ghost), and edited hundreds of financially and often critically successful stories people had told me, and I coauthored one bestseller myself. Eighty-six percent of the books I'd shepherded into the marketplace were profitable, compared to a less than forty percent success rate by the major traditional publishing houses.

What I'd learned that others ignored is that the complex stories, the mythic ones, are "true," meaning they resonate as absolutely consistent with real-life experience. The others—the overly chaotic or overly ordered ones, the propaganda ones—are false. They can seem true, like a very well-told lie, but are "false." Or as philosopher Harry Frankfurt technically categorized them, they're bullshit.

Simple as that.

So the time had come to fully commit to my internal editor, whom I'd come to trust as my means to distinguish authentic, earnest propositions from manipulative lies. My bullshit detector.

And my experience commercially exploiting that editor in the shadows would have to guide the next chapter of my own, teaching others how to transform their stories that were bullshit and "didn't work" into ones that weren't bullshit and "did work." If I could teach what I knew to others...more bullshit would be detected in the world, and more truth could then result.

Based on this stranger's complex story, the one he presented in his book and course, I trusted that he was telling me the truth about what he knew and did not know about how and why people chose to embark on transformational investigations. That's fancy talk for the simple act of spending time reading a blog post and then coming back to read the next one.

After all, opening oneself up to new information that can level up understanding is the birth of transformation. If there was no new information—no alternative signaling about the gravity of storytelling—then transformational bullshit detection would be impossible. I had the information about how to build bullshit detectors. I just needed to broadcast it.

Here, I thought, was another person who openly expressed exactly what he thought was the honorable way to build an audience, to virtuously send out signals. Plus, he did so without making promises he couldn't possibly keep. In fact, he repeatedly warned that creating a website was in no way a "get-rich-quick scheme." The long, hard slog could prove financially draining, so one should enter the arena for reasons beyond getting rich. Chances were, you wouldn't, so you needed another motivation to drive your commitment.

"This force which you didn't ask for, and this destiny which you must accept, is also your responsibility. And if you survive it, if you don't cheat, if you don't lie, it is not only, you know, your glory, your achievement, it is almost our only hope..."

— James Baldwin

I also liked the fact that I was no one special to him. My identity and reputation made no difference to what he presented. Anyone else who bought his book and took his class got the same information I did. He didn't seem to have "the real truth" hidden away, only available to big players capable of backchanneling shortcuts or writing bigger checks for the real easy, get-rich-quick stuff.

I was just as much of a rando to him as he was to me. So I handed over my $917, and he told me with clarity and conviction what he thought it took to attract attention authentically on the internet circa 2014.

I did what he advised, and here's the first post from that fall, Friday, September 19, 2014.

THE STORY GRID

What Good Editors Know

HOME ABOUT RESOURCES

What an Editor Does

by Shawn Coyne | 12 Comments

When a person meets me for the first time and learns that I make my living as a literary editor, the first question he invariably asks is:

> *"What exactly is it that you do?"*

The book I'm writing, *The Story Grid: What Good Editors Know*, and this website is the long answer.

The short answer is this:

When a manuscript that intrigues me arrives, I read it. I don't take notes. I just read it. If I finish the entire book—twenty four times out of twenty-five, I'll abandon it early on as the obvious work of an amateur—I will start to think seriously about its publishability. Does it work? Will it sell?

My editorial juices have started flowing now. Already I'm beginning to analyze and break down the manuscript's narrative. My decades of experience are telling me where, more or less, the Story is working and where it is not.

So far my process is identical to that of every other professional editor. But now, at this stage, I'll do something that no one else does.

I will run the manuscript through *The Story Grid.*

I'll do this as deeply as necessary and as many times as necessary to identify the problems, to evolve suggested solutions, to hone the story and shape it and elevate it to the highest level of storytelling craft.

Over a twenty-five year career as an editor and independent publisher (as well as a writer, agent, and manager) I've used this method to bring hundreds of works from raw manuscripts into A-level published fiction and non-fiction. Books that I have edited and published have grossed more than a hundred and fifty million dollars in North America alone. But more importantly, these books have changed people. They've changed the lives of readers and they've revolutionized the lives of the writers who authored them.

The Story Grid is a tool. It's a technique. It can't make something out of nothing, but it can make something out of almost-something, out of not-quite-something, out of two-inches-away-from-something. And it can inspire a work from idea to first draft.

What *The Story Grid* offers is a way for you, the writer, to evaluate whether or not your Story is working at the level of a publishable professional. If it is, *The Story Grid* will make it even better. If it isn't, *The Story Grid* will show you where and why it isn't working—and how to fix what's broken.

What follows in the days, weeks, months and years to come is how you can become your own editor.

Help Me, Help You!

Enter your email and join THE STORY GRID editorial department. You'll get free access to all of THE STORY GRID resources as I build them, one or two posts per week dedicated to the editing process and a ton of other stuff I haven't figured out yet.

* = required field

Email Address *

First Name

Last Name

Sign Me Up

- RSS - Posts
- RSS - Comments

Archives

Select Month

III

Middle of the Road
New York, New York, September 19, 2024
6:36 a.m.

After rereading that first post, it's a good sign that I still stand by what I wrote back then.

Obviously, there's much more to say about the evolution of *The Story Grid Methodology* into *The Story Grid Universe Theory*, as anyone who has taken one of my online courses will attest. But it remains clear that learning how to edit stories and eventually understanding what editors do (transformation of internal and external narration for the better or worse) is the pathway to fixing what's broken (false) and bettering what's working (true) in one's personal and shared worldviews.

After spending the last several years discovering the convergences between coherent science, spirituality, and philosophical traditions through Story Grid's lens, I now know that storytelling is far more universal than I'd previously realized.

Before there was spirituality, philosophy, or science, there was storytelling. It is the root tautology behind existential evolution (the abstract universe), environmental ecology (the interpretive world), and cognitive development (the conceptual cosmos). All ecological parts are observers who tell stories, knowingly or unknowingly, and the whole of those parts is greater than their sum. I subscribe to physicist and philosopher John Archibald Wheeler's interpretation of quantum information theory as the emergence of the participatory universe. As such, I understand that all observable phenomena are themselves observers.

Observers make sense of the universe by following universal narrative patterns (macro phase shifts, meso threshold crossings, and micro transition bridges), again knowingly or unknowingly. My favorite coffee mug, in all likelihood, does not "know" it's undergoing transformational degradations that follow dissipative patterns, but it does so nevertheless. The power inherent in understanding these patterns is immeasurable. Simply, stories structure all that is, was, and ever will be.

So what's all the hullaballoo? Obviously, you don't need to understand the internal combustion engine to drive a car, and you technically don't need to understand my theory to tell a story. So why am I writing this "mission statement"?

I need to publicly declare the importance of my life's work and accept that my declaration will invite ever more dismissive "everyone knows storytelling is subjective" wave-aways about my conclusions.

I won't just receive those barbs from the usual suspects—the literary professionals and the mistaken folk wisdom they spread in the culture to aspiring writers looking for magic or formulas. It's probable I'll get them from contemporary scientists, spiritualists, and philosophers whom I respect. But I also understand that chances are they won't even consider my work at all, instinctually concluding from my premise that it's unworthy of investigation. After all, there are no "Story departments" at universities or any metaphorical acknowledgment that—as water is to fish, the air is to birds, the earth is to worms—the story is to *be*. My axiomatic proposition that storytelling is akin to the abstract science described by Claude Shannon's Mathematical Theory of Communication, the intellectual substrate of the digital information age, has yet to be fully appreciated. But it's time it should be.

It's difficult, too, as the people closest to me, who aren't contributing to Story Grid but admire my passion and zeal for the project, aren't convinced I know what I speak of either. They've also been implanted with the same "everyone knows storytelling is subjective" protocol. My explanations require such an extensive survey of the collective cultural grammar from antiquity to the present day that I exhaust their patience quickly. Just as I'm probably exhausting yours now with all of my Hamlet-esque dithering.

What does any of this have to do with you?

Hopefully, once these findings are well-understood and spread, no one will be thinking about me and my life's work. The recurring narrative patterns are so self-evident that any claim I "invented" them is ridiculous. If anyone codified the molten core of my theory, it was a guy who lived twenty-five hundred years ago—Aristotle in his *Poetics*. All I've done is clarify the essence of his understanding into actionable steps and choices one can use to make sense of the world.

But make no mistake, his and my findings require an educational reconfiguration. We need to stop teaching people how to "write" convincing arguments and begin to teach them how to tell and perform complex, mythic stories. In other words, we need to teach people how to "author."

"The truth does not change according to our ability to stomach it."

— Flannery O'Connor

I know the long-term effects of this return to Aristotle's four-causal framework and conformity theory will be well worth it, but the short-term turbulence we'll need to weather—the inevitable resistance to its adoption—is not insignificant.

To tell better stories—from the micro bottom to the meso middle, up to the macro top, and through the meta whole—we'll need to add another layer to our pedagogy and upturn the tables of what we earnestly believed was the way forward before.

IV

Changes
Nashville, Tennessee, November 7, 2024
9:18 a.m.

The only way to level up physically, psychologically, metaphysically, and behaviorally as an artist (another word for a creative being, i.e., you) is to turn and face the strange. We must undergo a painful personal four-part transformation. And the only way to leave a compelling, cathartic, meaningful, and lasting legacy is to express those four painful life-changing revelations by telling a mythic story that's "not about you" but about "what's in you."

Why?

Because what's in you is also in me, and your cousin Larry, and your stepsister Phyllis, and any being with the ability to make choices, for that matter. We share that dynamic core stuff, and the only way through this difficult life is by knowing and understanding in the depths of ourselves that we are not alone. Everyone is torn asunder by paradox. No one is immune to the polarities of experience.

Seriously.

What's required of us all is to tell a complex story by acting out and authoring a mythic one.

What's a mythic story? It's one that is more true than the quotidian and mind-numbingly boring reality of everyday existence. It's a synoptic integration of the big moments of one's life distilled into a seamless sequence of escalatingly meaningful happenstance. It's the kind of story that we hear, read, watch, whatever, and our jaws drop, awestruck at the authenticity of the translation of someone's obvious insight into the human condition. We don't question that the author was telling us their honest-to-God truth. The work leaves us stunned...both in pity of the poor protagonist who suffered through the events and fearful of our falling into the same vortex. We are purged of emotion. That's what Aristotle meant by catharsis. Aristotle's father was a doctor, and catharsis is a medical term that means "to purge."

It's important to note that a mythic story doesn't mean that you'll "like it." There are more mythic stories to tell than we can even begin to imagine. Some of them will speak to you. Some of them won't. But what they all have in common is that you can't help but finish them to find out what happens. How did the story resolve itself? If you can write a mythic story, you will find an audience. And of that audience, many of them will reach catharsis. They will be released from feeling alone. They will bind to you and be thankful for your authorial authenticity.

This is what Story Grid is all about.

To tell and author such a story requires metaphorically reaching down into ourselves and finding the profound truths and falsities of one of a series of disturbing and resonant experiences by exploring the possibility that you've misunderstood your triumphs as failures and failures as triumphs.

'Cause guess what? You have. That is the paradoxical truth in all its beauty. For all appearance of wins, there are hidden losses, and for all appearance of loss, there are hidden wins.

To author such a mythic story requires a personal mapping of universal territory. The author must map the situation they're portraying to an analogous experience in their personal history.

Without personal mapping, a story is inauthentic (that means not mythic, not truer than true), no matter how well-written or crafted. It's—excuse the expression and again, using Harry Frankfurt's technical definition—bullshit.

Mythic stories are true and require authentic expression of personal experience. Bullshit stories are false and are inauthentic expressions of non-realized experience—fake.

V

Wonderful World
Nashville, Tennessee, November 8, 2024
3:47 p.m.

Story Grid refuses to teach bullshit generation and propagation.

Instead, all true story-gridders must undergo the four storyteller transformations. For once they've crossed the final Rubicon—the holistic leap from inauthentic to authentic—they will have the power to tell and enact mythic stories worthy of their individual and our collective being.

VI

Wake Up Time
Delta Flight 3815, November 9, 2024
11:13 a.m.

Personal mapping is the deep work we all need to embrace so we can coherently share the truth as we know it in communion with the big truth as we desire it.

What big truth do we desire?

It is the continuance of all that is, was, and ever will be after we are no longer privileged to be participants in it. In other words, we want whatever experience we're all sharing and exploring together to carry on after we're gone. We want it to continue. It's meaningful and important.

Why?

Because it's heartbreaking and enlightening and compelling and unjust and all those other qualities, quantities, and relationships we can't quite put our finger on and name. It's simply unbelievable to be able to be a part of this wonderful mess. To get to care about others and things is divine. You obviously care or you wouldn't desire to become an author.

> **"Apart from Beauty, Truth is neither good, nor bad... Truth matters because of beauty."**
>
> **— Alfred North Whitehead**

I can no longer soft-pedal this difficult and painful process—personal mapping of universal experience—or gloss over it.

It is absolutely necessary for the continuance of whatever this is.

Fear of financial, relational, and intellectual retribution is not justification for not standing by the truth.

We can't hide our love away anymore. We have to express it in mythic story, or the bullshit stories will devour us and destroy what's left of whatever this is. What I have in mind isn't a course, a pathway that most people are interested in. They say they are, but when it comes to actually doing the work necessary to overcome intransigent obstacles, they balk.

As Friedrich Hegel said of Immanuel Kant, "He won't get into the water until he knows how to swim." You'll never know how to swim, of course, unless you get in the water. What's required to map personal experience onto a universal mythic pattern then is to just keep getting in the water...to keep imitating the patterns until they become your own.

Most people are really interested in reaching some idyllic utopic promised land in the future or returning to a former idyllic promised land in the past. And they're looking for minimal personal/emotional investment in that journey.

I can assure you that neither the future utopia nor past nostalgia is attainable, and anyone who says otherwise is bullshitting you. Those who sell such nonsense are either naive, duplicitous, or both. No magically chosen people are gifted storytelling as a superpower, and no formula will make you one without undergoing the four transformations. One can only follow these four transformational processes and their recurring patterns to realize one's authentic narrative and leave a legacy of truth.

No authentic transformation, no truth. Simple as that.

VII

Everything I Am Is Yours
New York, New York November 9, 2024 through Present

I'm not saying anything I haven't said before.

It's just more urgent now.

We are swimming in bullshit, and we need bullshit detectors to sort through the malicious flotsam and jetsam to negotiate through the real, paradoxical transcendences.

What are these transcendences? They are spectral admixtures that cannot be reduced to one or the other.

Good and evil, the physical laws of unintended consequences. All gains require losses.

Beauty and ugliness, the psychological rules of resonant dissonance. All attractions require repulsions.

Truth and falsity, the metaphysical principles of coherent conjecture. All certainties require unprovability.

Authenticity and inauthenticity, the holistic dynamics of manifest identities. All actions require performances.

What do the four transformations have to do with it? The four transformations empower higher order negotiation of the four transcendences.

Conceptually, transformation is a pretty straightforward process to understand.

Here's the macro version. Just three phase-shift steps generate the simplest behavioral complexity.

Beginning: I behave one way to get something.

Middle: An event happens as a result, which encourages (it works, and I get what I want) or discourages (it doesn't work, and I don't get what I want) my behavior and then—

End: I behave differently.

The beginning, middle, and end are the phase shifts.

Let's drill down to the meso level. Just six threshold-crossing steps generate behavioral novelty.

Origin: an originating desire to attain a goal, like authoring a story, to—

Incitement: the inciting birth of skill acquisition (deliberate practice, writing small stories, and getting feedback on them) to—

Criticality: ever more critical suffering from obstacles and failures to attain those skills (lots of failures, like so many it can feel impossible) which reach a turning point, a revelation/realization/insight in which—

Crisis: a crisis sacrifice of a tightly held previously adaptive habit must be chosen (like insisting that you don't have to think about your life to write compelling scenes) to—

Climax: the climactic death of that old way of being (you begin to map your life to your fiction) and lastly, inevitably—

Resolution: the becoming of a new form, the resolute rebirth of a fresh desire to attain a new goal (string together a sequence of scenes that become greater than the sum of their parts).

The threshold crossings are original desire, inciting birth, critical suffering, crisis sacrifice, climax death, and resolution resurrection.

The micro level consists of nine transition-bridging steps that generate complex behavioral simplicity.

Locality: Establish "where you are" in the process, your position learning about the work. Are you in the early "know-nothing" stage, the middle "know-a-little" stage, or the upper "know-a-lot" stage? Are you willing to rethink your position?

Temporality: Establish the "when you are" in the process, your momentum state doing the work. Are you flustered and want to move slower, frustrated and want to move faster, or in a Goldilocks flow-state momentum? What are you willing to do to rethink your momentum?

Modality: Establish the "how you are" in the process. Are you receptive to feedback, critical of feedback, or overwhelmed by feedback? What are you willing to do to rethink your approach to feedback?

Content: Establish the "what is in play" in the process. Are you attracted to particular kinds of material and repulsed by others? What are you willing to do to rethink your approach to what you work on?

Context: Establish the "where and when" of your process. Are you attracted to particular arenas—settings, situations, constraints—and repulsed by others? What are you willing to do to rethink your approach to the worlds you choose?

Conduct: Establish the "how it acts" in your process. Are you attracted to particular patterns of behavior and repulsed by others? What are you willing to do to rethink your assumptions about how things move and act?

Identity: Establish the "who you are" in the process. Do you define yourself as a particular stylist (literary, bare-bones, commercial, etc.)? What are you willing to do to rethink your approach to your style?

Intention: Establish the "why you are" in the process. Do you have a particular cause or no cause to communicate? What are you willing to do to rethink your approach to controlling ideas?

Significance: Establish the "what you are" in the process. Do you have a coherent worldview to rely upon, or do you rely upon others' worldviews? What are you willing to do to rethink your approach to essences?

Transition bridges include locality, temporality, modality, content, context, conduct, identity, intention, and significance.

Knowing about the three phase shifts, the six threshold crossings, and the nine transition bridges seems enough to generate believable simulations of macro, meso, and micro transformations.

Are they enough, though?

While extraordinarily helpful in identifying particular story problems, what I've described above cannot reliably convey the essence of transformation. The nine micro transitions are akin to organization, the six thresholds are akin to the structure, and the three phases are akin to the function, but without an essence, they do not produce real change.

Huh?

When we practice transformation, changing one's behavior—growing oneself—hurts in every way imaginable: physically, psychologically, metaphysically, and especially publicly. As George Bernard Shaw wrote, "Hell is full of musical amateurs."

As someone who has spent much of my professional life in the company of storytelling amateurs, I can assure you that transforming from an amateur to an author is as difficult, if not more so, than learning an instrument.

We need to recognize that extreme difficulty and encourage our students to keep at it, especially when it begins to hurt publicly. We also need to make the process more enjoyable, less serious, and continually remind everyone that what we write when we're practicing is not precious.

Let me be more specific regarding the four transformational skills necessary to become a storytelling authority.

Physical transformation is about reading and describing how changes occur in the environment. It involves transmitting motion information with micro efficiency. It is about improving one's on-the-surface, line-by-line sentence generation with minimum viable wordage for maximal energetic effect. The micro conveyance of locality, temporality, modality, content, context, conduct, identity, intention, and significance of a single event resides here.

Psychological transformation is about writing and explaining how change occurs in the real world. It involves meaningfully translating emotion with meso empathy. It is about improving one's beyond-the-surface conveyance of the six must-haves that connote meaningful change: (1) originating desire (2) inciting interaction (3) critical turning point (4) crisis choice (5) the climactic action (6) resolution response in a single event that can eventually scale into a higher-order meaning as a sequence of events.

Metaphysical transformation is about editing and defining how change occurs in the ideological world. It involves representing symbolic behaviors that order commotion with macro anticipation. It embeds one's above-the-surface ultimate relative concern via beginning, middle, and ending conventions and obligatory moments (story constraints) with specific emphasis on one of the six general blueprint genres in all complex stories: (1) Horror (2) Love (3) Action (4) Status (5) Morality (6) Worldview.

Holistic transformation is about authoring and demonstrating how change occurs in real life. It involves the pragmatic realization of a new behavioral pathway the creator has authentically undergone in their personal history. It requires mapping one's personal experience as a traumatized and persistent presence in the existential universe onto the imaginal avatars at play in the author's transcendent (mythic—more real than real) story.

I realize now that the ominous feeling ten years after my launch of www.storygrid.com, the hour of darkness presaging the light, was about this final holistic transformation.

Should Story Grid insist that our students undergo this final holistic transformation before declaring them capable and powerful authors who authentically present the truth as they know it?

That is, should we insist that all Story Grid graduates become authors who write complex mythic stories and not bullshit ones?

To find out whether this Story Grid way of seeing transformation was real and reliable, I had to test it against the best stories told in science, spirituality, philosophy, and narrative theory.

ARTWORK BY MASAMITSU SHIGETA

VIII

Authority Song
New York, New York November 9, 2024 through Present

The past years since stepping away from the day-to-day operations of the company, I've synthesized my global narrative theory, **Story Grid Universe Theory**, testing its convergence with a slew of scientific, spiritual, philosophical, and storytelling frameworks. To say the work has been fruitful would be an understatement.

My goal was to align my work such that it converges with the preeminent works of contemporary and classical cognitive science, depth psychology, theology, and systems thinking, including:

John Vervaeke's Relevance Realization Theory.

Karl Friston's Free Energy Principle and Predictive Processing / Active Inference Theory.

Chris Fields' quantum-information-theoretic interpretation of Friston's work, Chris Fuchs's Quantum Bayesian framework, and John Archibald Wheeler's Participatory Universe Theory.

Carl Jung's Depth Psychology and Individuation Process.

Paul Tillich's *The Courage to Be* / Ultimate Concern framework.

Michael Levin's Cognitive Light Cone Theory.

Claude Shannon's Information Theory.

John von Neumann's Automata Theory.

Alicia Juarrero's Complex Dynamical Systems Theory.

Norbert Wiener's Cybernetics Theory.

Newell and Simon's Search/Inference framework.

Joseph Campbell's *Hero's Journey* framework.

And, the inspiring work that started it all, Aristotle's *Poetics*.

Story Grid Universe Theory is a convergence argument that presupposes that there is **natural truth** (a leveled ontology) and **reality**, and that we can get closer to both by probing (a conformity epistemology) the universe, world, and cosmos with broad and deep relational exploration—finding the connections between one pattern and another. That is another way of describing what I mean by **mapping personal experience to universal patterns.**

> **"They must be considered strangers to the truth, who do no more than daydream about the nature of truth, fashioning it more to their own fancy than according to knowledge."**
>
> **— Clement of Alexandria**

I'm currently writing up my findings. *Mentoring the Machines*, which I'm coauthoring with John Vervaeke, is close to completion. Once I've wrapped that project, I'll begin what I'm tentatively calling *Principia Mythica*, which will build the entire Story Grid theory and methodology from first principles.

These past few months have completely transformed the way I see the world. I'm convinced my work will aid other meaning-makers too.

What's the gist of my findings?

Fragmented thinking, as represented by the tyrannical stories told today as ultimate truths, is causing us as a collective post-modern culture to fundamentally misunderstand reality. We've lost the through-line meaningful whole and have fallen prey to incomplete particulars.

That is, the majority of scientists, spiritualists, philosophers, and story-tellers mistake **parts** of manifest reality for the **integrated whole** of reality. They fall in love with their theories, doctrines, paradigms, and pragmatics and find themselves cognitively straight-jacketed. Their commitment to their particular investigative channel blinds them to other valid perspectives and undermines their innate capacity to change their minds.

Thus, we are besieged with physical reductionists, psychological dogmatists, philosophical idealists, and storytelling absurdists who vehemently insist on their certainty and fundamental unconditional correctness. Their demanding our adoption of their conclusions as sacrosanct and incontrovertible is tearing apart the civility of society. To disagree or even to question these authorities is verboten.

After exhaustive research and consideration, I've come to the following conclusions:

No single **theory of everything** can be derived from scientific investigation. Kurt Gödel and Karl Popper settled this notion quite some time ago using the very methods of science to do so.

No single **doctrine of everyone** can be derived from spiritual investigation. Carl Jung's investigation of spiritual traditions through the ages resulted in his recognition of recurring patterns across civilizations he called archetypes. These archetypes fluctuate within and without our worlds vying for our attention and manifestation. There is no single archetype but a dynamic of contradictory polarity—anima/animus or dissipation/conservation—in all systems. John Vervaeke describes these as opponent processes.

No single **paradigm of every agent** can be derived from philosophical investigation. Each agent's model of reality is uniquely theirs. No two observers "see" the same way, but that doesn't mean they're not seeing anything. There is no ideal form, no "view from nowhere," as William James and Thomas Nagel elegantly argue.

No single **behavior of every actor** can be derived from story investigation. Each actor's way of being is uniquely theirs and can only be described, explained, defined, and demonstrated as their particular procedural performance. There is no perfect set of actions, as there are no perfect actors. There can be no perfect action because of the invariance of variance as a fundamental first principle of manifest reality.

What Story Grid Universe Theory proposes instead is that none of these three parts of experience—the physical universe, the psychological world, and the metaphysical cosmos—is more real than the others. The whole of reality emerges from their synoptic integration into a complex story that is greater than the sum of its parts, and storytelling is the way we participate in, perceive, and perform that whole.

IX

We Used to Wait
New York, New York March 17, 2026

The Story Grid Universe Theory proposes—in its implicit essence—that storytelling is not a magical gift that only a select few possess but a deeply patterned formal faculty that anyone who dedicates themselves to recognizing and practicing those patterns can master.

The core proposition remains that once an aspiring storyteller understands the universal forms of the patterns, and they can clearly signal their own particular pattern in tune with those universal forms, they have the potential to compel a reader to sense, feel, think, and become transformed. That is, they can change the way they sense things, feel about relationships, and think about ideas to become their authentic selves.

Again, I still stand by that simple complexity.

Storytelling is a deliberate skill acquisition process, not a genetic predisposition.

In other words, storytelling is learned.

And just as scientific theory, spiritual doctrine, and philosophical paradigm can be studied and understood, so can storytelling pragmatics. In fact, it is the "one practice" science, spirituality, and philosophy all have in common. Without storytelling, we wouldn't have science, spirituality, or philosophy. It's the boot-strapping process for all of the parts of the whole.

The very good news is that you don't either "have storytelling capacity" or "don't have it." The innate potential within all beings can become actualized. And—ask any scientist, spiritualist, or philosopher, who will all tell you the same thing—the way potential becomes actualized is via emergent transformation.

Just as one undergoes a transformation from a fertilized egg to a newborn being to a child and then to an adolescent, an adult, and hopefully a sage, so can one transform from an incoherent and noisy storyteller to a coherent and clear one.

You have already seen this transformational pattern in outline. Here is the more complete version and how it converges with science, spirituality, and philosophy.

I argue that transformations of our observational species (as well as all other observers in the universe) mirror Story Grid Universe Theory's three-six-nine, macro-meso-micro structure.

Here's the abstract cheat sheet, which I've adapted from the earlier narrative version.

There are three phase shifts, macro stages of a system's internality, understanding, and solving commotion—problem solving.

Complexity.

Chaos.

Order.

There are six threshold crossings, meso states of mediating between the internal and the external, knowing and managing emotion—game playing.

An originating desire to change the game.

The birth of the process to actualize the change.

The suffering of doing what's necessary to make the process a habit.

The sacrifice of other possibilities to enable the prioritization of that habit.

The death of parts of the system's former self (old habit/s) when the system enacts the new habit/s.

The resurrection as transformed systems who have become something they'd never been before (a new habit) at the expense of what they once were (an old habit).

There are nine transition bridges, micro scales of externality, sensing, and directing motion—noise navigating.

Locality: Where is the motion?

Temporality: When is the motion?

Modality: How is the motion?

Content: What kind of agent is in motion?

Context: What kind of arena surrounds that agent in motion?

Conduct: How does that agent typically move and act within that arena?

Identity: Who is the motion—what archetypal "who" is being enacted?

Intention: Why is the motion—what archetypal aim is driving it?

Significance: What does this motion ultimately mean—what archetypal pattern does it realize?

"I am not cruel — only truthful."

— Sylvia Plath

I call the macro structure above-the-surface. Scientists, spiritualists, and philosophers have other names for it. The scientist refers to the macro realm as cognition. The spiritualist calls it the transcendent cosmos. And the philosopher calls it conditional reasoning. Everyday people call it thinking and problem-solving.

I call the meso structure beyond-the-surface. Scientists, spiritualists, and philosophers have other names for it. The scientist refers to the meso realm as consciousness. The spiritualist calls it the experiential world. And the philosopher calls it rationality. Everyday people call it feeling and game-playing.

I call the micro structure on-the-surface. Scientists, spiritualists, and philosophers have other names for it. The scientist refers to the micro realm as sentience. The spiritualist calls it the existential universe. And the philosopher calls it intelligence. Everyday people call it sensing and noise-navigating.

Just to tie off this bundle of concepts, Story Grid Universe Theory proposes that the three meta-parts, which we can think of as macro philosophy, meso spirituality, and micro science, are consistent and convergent with my concepts of above-the-surface, beyond-the-surface, and on-the-surface storytelling.

The kicker, as you may have already surmised, is that a whole story is the simultaneous distillation and synthesis (synoptic integration) of these three parts into a whole greater than their sum. It's the higher order union of simple complexity, medial novel co-creation, and complex simplicity.

Previously I've labeled this analytical realm over-neath-the-surface, but I'm leaning toward changing that name to **through-the-surfaces**. This final cause can be understood as reality writ large, or shared reality. Shared reality is what actually happens that is observed as a manifest event by multiple observers.

My coauthor John Vervaeke describes my on-the-surface plane of reality as participatory knowing, beyond-the-surface as perspectival knowing, above-the-surface as propositional knowing, and my through-the-surfaces as procedural knowing.

Thus, we need to understand the totality of experience (the individual and the whole) in terms of a whole made up of three parts (these are the levels of ontology), and not as a single part (that is an individual epistemology) that is the whole. This is what I mean by mistaking a part (one epistemology) of the whole for the whole (the path integral of all epistemologies that comprise ontology).

What do all of these egg-heady abstractions have to do with Story Grid and my dark night of the soul?

A lot.

You see, another way of thinking about these big concepts is:

Science is about reading the physical universe, or indexing observations, making sense of good and evil, and the axiom "All gains require loss."

Spirituality is about writing the psychological world, framing measurements, making meaning of beauty and ugliness, and the axiom "All attractions require repulsions."

Philosophy is about editing the metaphysical cosmos, modeling predictions, making understanding of truth and falsity, and the axiom "All certainties require unprovability (faith)."

Storytelling is about authoring the manifest reality, shaping transformations, making behavior of authenticity and inauthenticity, and the axiom "All actions require performances."

Let's circle back to what I wrote earlier about those four kinds of transformations a cohesive storyteller needs to undergo to discover, explore, operationalize, and express how to show someone else what they've been through.

Physical transformation is about reading and describing how changes occur in the environment. It involves transmitting motion information with micro efficiency. It is about improving one's on-the-surface, line-by-line sentence generation with minimum viable wordage for maximal energetic effect. The micro conveyance of locality, temporality, modality, content, context, conduct, identity, intention, and significance of a single event resides here.

Psychological transformation is about writing and explaining how change occurs in the real world. It involves meaningfully translating emotion with meso empathy. It is about improving one's beyond-the-surface conveyance of the six must-haves that connote meaningful change: (1) originating desire (2) inciting interaction (3) critical turning point (4) crisis choice (5) the climactic action (6) resolution response in a single event (and, by extension, a sequence of events).

Metaphysical transformation is about editing and defining how change occurs in the ideological world. It involves representing symbolic behaviors that order commotion with macro anticipation. It embeds one's above-the-surface ultimate relative concern via beginning, middle, and ending conventions and obligatory moments with specific emphasis on one of the six general blueprint genres in all complex stories: (1) Horror (2) Love (3) Action (4) Status (5) Morality (6) Worldview.

Holistic transformation is about authoring and demonstrating how change occurs in real life. It involves the pragmatic realization of a new behavioral pathway the creator has authentically undergone in their personal history. It requires mapping one's personal experience as a traumatized and persistent presence in the existential universe onto the imaginal avatars at play in the author's transcendent (mythic—more real than real) story.

"A lie is profanity. A lie is the worst thing in the world. Art is the ability to tell the truth."

— Richard Pryor

So this kind of pragmatic transformation can be thought of in mythic storytelling terms because mythic storytelling is about authoring the manifestation of reality and shaping transformations—behavior-making.

In other words, the Story Grid Way is not an outlier but a through-the-surfaces integration of science, spirituality, philosophy, and storytelling—a way of seeing reality that is commensurate with, and capable of coordinating, all of their siloed insights.

X

I Believe in You
September 19, 2024, 8:57 a.m.

Ten years after its founding, Story Grid released a novel called *The Shithead*, the proof of concept for *The Story Grid Methodology*. A ten-year project requiring multiple cycles of transformation from both the author and the editorial mentor, the results are emblematic of a **reader-to-writer-to-editor-to-author transformation.** In Story Grid Universe terms, that means he traversed the full three phase shifts, six thresholds, and nine trasition bridges, culminating in a through-the-surfaces, holistic transformation.

I advise anyone interested in *The Story Grid* to read that novel. If you don't find it has compelling narrative drive, complex emotional breadth and depth, or a cathartic resolution, you will likely not buy into my four-transformation proposal.

That doesn't mean you must think it's the best story ever written or an irresistible bestseller. Those are not Story Grid indexes. As stated earlier, mythic stories are concrete examples of laser-focused universal human behavioral patterns. One person's difficulty recognizing a particular pattern may not be another's. So one person's definition of a masterwork is another's "I think it was good but not as good as X, Y, or Z." This phenomenon is simply because the paradox at the story's center isn't something that confounds you personally. In this way, and only this way, is storytelling subjective.

What's essential, though, is to recognize the craft and the care the author has embedded in the narrative. If you don't think the author truly cared about what they were writing and authentically pursued a clear vision for the story's intended core audience—which, again, you may not be a part of—the process they used to create the story will likely not resonate with you.

You just have to recognize the story's singularity as a clear expression of the singular author's vision. The bottom line is what I call the **"Category of One"** feature. Is there any other book like it? Or is it uniquely the work of the author? Is the author's voice singular, or is it generic?

The critical litmus test is simple. Did you find yourself compelled to read the whole thing? If you did, that would mean you spent at least four hours of your life, depending upon how quickly you read, caring about the plight of an imaginary person. That is meaningful.

In fact, it's the core of meaning itself: caring about another being and wishing them the best or the worst, as the case may be. As Aristotle would say, those who can induce pity and fear for imaginary beings are poets. Spending four hours thinking about someone else, even someone who does not physically exist, is life-changing.

The Shithead is a novel that works on all three communication levels (Story Grid's **on-the-surface**, **beyond-the-surface**, and **above-the-surface**) and pays off as a dynamic whole greater than the sum of its three parts. This is what I call **through-the-surfaces** communication, a unique totality of experience. To tie these concepts back to our four transformations:

On-the-surface concerns **physical transformation**, a sense of motion.

Beyond-the-surface concerns **psychological transformation**, a meaningful emotion.

Above-the-surface concerns **metaphysical transformation**, an insightful commotion.

Through-the-surfaces concerns **holistic transformation**, a coherent promotion.

With time, reflection, and open intellectual curiosity, readers will eventually discover precisely what I mean by all of that. And with time, *The Shithead* will be one of those books, like *The War of Art*, that will bind strangers together in a shared worldview.

Even though a lot of people don't appreciate stories like *The Shithead* as I do, that's okay. Every mythic story isn't for everyone. But I care so deeply about the existential necessity of generating mythic complex storytelling that I will spend the rest of my professional life helping aspiring storytellers write more categories-of-one books like it. Their stories will capture the hardship, humor, and gravity of their particular ultimate concern. No one else could have written *The Shithead* but the author.

Anyway, what's important about the novel isn't just that it is our proof of concept. It's the identity of the author.

The author is the same guy who, ten years ago, charged me 917 dollars to learn how to start the website www.storygrid.com. He was the stranger I'd put my faith in to tell me the truth about how to start Story Grid. And in turn, he put his faith in me to teach him how to write a meaningful and compelling novel. Let me explain.

Nine months after I launched www.storygrid.com, I got an email from Tim Grahl, the author of *Your First 1,000 Copies*, the book I read in the summer of 2014 that encouraged me to launch a website dedicated to my theories. What I appreciated about that book was the specificity Grahl presented to actualize editor Kevin Kelly's seminal "1,000 True Fans" philosophy. Kelly is an influential and prophetic figure in digital publishing and commerce. He proselytized the long-tail marketplace as the future for individual intellectual property owners since the 1980s. As one of the beneficiaries of the long tail, he was absolutely correct.

According to his email, Grahl confessed that book marketing was his shadow career. What he really wanted to do was write novels. He explained that he had tried every "learn how to write" method, but none had transformed his prose. No matter how intently he followed writing advice, he couldn't write compelling fiction. He'd now read *The Story Grid* and thought that, at last, he'd found a way to reach his ambitions. But more importantly to me, he felt his idea could simultaneously expand The Story Grid's audience. Would I be willing to speak with him for half an hour?

Here's the thing. By the time Grahl emailed me, I'd sold close to five thousand copies of *The Story Grid* in just a few months, a very good start. As a result, I received many emails from people who read the book and wanted me to be their mentor. I begged off. At that point in my career, I'd had at least four experiences working with writers who could craft compelling sentences but couldn't tell a story with any facility. They falsely assumed that the storytelling part was an add-on to fluid line-by-line writing. But when push came to shove, they couldn't get over that whole "everyone knows that writing is subjective" meme they'd assumed to be accurate but never really examined. Ultimately, my arguments failed to convince them otherwise, and they abandoned their projects.

I didn't know what Mark Twain meant when he said, "Don't try and teach a pig to sing. It's a waste of your time, and it annoys the pig," until after those painful experiences. The thing is, though, we aren't pigs. We are human beings who, with time, can understand transcending ourselves via transformation. I'm betting on it.

Grahl was the only emailer who offered to help me in exchange for helping him—a reciprocal partnership. All the others simply focused on their desires and how I could help fulfill them, as if all editors are on Earth to serve writers. The other emailers asking for my help weren't interested in expanding the audience for *The Story Grid*, just their own.

And, of course, I knew Grahl as the guy I'd somewhat anonymously paid to help me launch the site, however tangentially.

We had our call, and his offer was simple. If I agreed to speak with him for an hour a week about writing, and if I would read his stuff that I would assign him to write and give him feedback about making it work, he'd create a podcast called *The Story Grid Podcast*. I would own and control the podcast. He'd do all the technical work. All I had to do in exchange was incrementally teach him how to write a novel.

I agreed under one condition. He had to do exactly what I told him to do. I was not interested if he half-assed the work or if he argued with me about concepts it had taken me twenty-plus years to formalize.

We launched the podcast in the fall of 2015, and it quickly became popular and a must-listen in aspirational writing circles.

The sales of *The Story Grid* book climbed. However, I discovered that while Tim understood the concepts in *The Story Grid*, he had trouble executing them. To put it bluntly, and I often did, he couldn't write coherent sentences. They were grammatically and syntactically "correct," but reading his work required tremendous energy. They were so dull and generic it was excruciating to get through them.

Evaluating it was painstaking, and I found myself writing more commentary about his work than the work itself. He just wasn't getting better.

Not a good sign.

But I'd made him a promise. I'd agreed to do my best to teach him how to write compelling stories people would read and tell their friends about. I arrogantly didn't think doing that would be so difficult.

Boy, was I wrong. What I thought wouldn't take longer than a couple of years took a decade. The good news is that we captured everything we learned about teaching storytelling, and we continue to improve the process. What took Grahl ten years we estimate will take other aspiring authors three and a half. Maybe eventually less. We're still working on it!

You see, I had no intention of transforming my life's work in the "marketing" process of selling it, but it soon became apparent that I'd have to.

My top-down thirty-thousand-foot viewpoint—while sensible, reasonable, and coherent as an analytical tool for those who desired to become professional editors—was not all that effective for aspiring writers.

And if the editor cannot explain and mentor the writer from a "nonworking story" to a "working story" with grace and a clear, proven pathway for success, then editor/writer relationships are bound to remain fragmented and mercurial. After all, if the editor couldn't understand the writer's experience, and the writer couldn't understand what the editor was asking them to do—like two caring adults who spoke different languages but wished to help one another—they'd never truthfully integrate into a cooperative, coherent whole.

I was used to receiving manuscripts that were "close to working" or unsalvageable but well-written. Still, the writers who'd made it to my inbox certainly knew basic scene-writing skills. Some of their scenes didn't work, but many of them did.

What was troubling was that I wrote *The Story Grid* to present my methodology not just as an editing tool but as a reverse-engineering tool. In other words, I believed it could empower writers to transform a juicy narrative idea into a working story. Once they understood story structure—the recurring patterns of real intelligibility—they'd be set, I naively proposed.

I know now there is a vertigo-inducing chasm, a significant and vital difference between being a "writer" and a "storyteller." It's like standing on a ledge and wanting to reach another higher level that seems impossibly far away. The first three transformations we teach at Story Grid (the on-the-surface, beyond-the-surface, and above-the-surface) get you to the edge of the ledge, but the only way to make it to the higher level is through-the-surfaces. And while I can easily tell you what to do to get there—mapping your personal story patterns to the universal story patterns—only you can make it happen. It's the throughline meta-threshold. And the only way across it is to take a running start, leaping, falling, getting back up and doing it again. And again and again, until you make it. You will make it. And when you do, you'll know what I mean about bullshit stories and mythic authentic ones.

Again, you'll inevitably fall, and you'll have to dust yourself off and climb back up the mountain to try again and…fall again. Who knows how many leaps it will take you to reach the other side, but once you do, you won't need me or anyone else to tell you that you are an authoritative and authentic storyteller. You'll know it in the depths of your soul and the ever-expanding breadth of your vision.

This is the **holistic transformation,** the threshold of thresholds. We who care about communicating truth know it is the one you must cross to attain meaningful commercial success. We want that for you, and we will continue to pursue the best practices that empower you to seize it yourself.

Now that I know the differences between readers, writers, editors, and authors, it is clear that our world does not need more verbiage. It requires more authoritative and authentic storytellers.

To be a complex storyteller certainly relies upon the reader, writer, and editor skill sets. However, having those three as separate truncated operations is insufficient to become a complex, path-integrated storyteller.

Faith and empathy are required to make the final holistic transformation. Faith and empathy for oneself first and then extending that faith and empathy to fictional avatars via mapping a personal experience onto a contrived scenario.

ILLUSTRATION BY VICTOR JUHASZ

Let's unpack this idea a bit more.

A skilled writer can make a compelling argument and often convince an audience that they have a unique and "special/more enlightened" worldview. They are, in essence, "better" or more attuned and sensitive than the reader, that their writerly point of view is "right," and the reader—until they've been enlightened by the brilliant presentation of the writer—is "wrong."

These writers wish to be placed on a pedestal and considered magical "artists" who can transport readers to other worlds and show and tell them things they, the reader, could never have imagined.

These writers are not so interested in conveying a deep, meaningful human experience as they are in presenting themselves as "above the fray" with a "god-like" vision that can see through human comedy and tragedy. They are the knowers. And their readers are the not-know-ers.

These writers are above it all and can enlighten only those with the intellectual or visceral capacity to appreciate their genius—their subjects. Do you see how the whole "storytelling is just subjective" proposition we were taught in school contemptuously bottoms out? It's a contempt for the reader as a sentient, conscious, cognitive, and creative being. They are simply the "consumer" of the writer's magic.

It's been my experience that these writers, once they've made their mark, resist recognizing the meaning of recurring multifaceted universal/world-ly/cosmological patterns. Instead, they mistake one part of that trinity—the physical universe, the psychological world, or the metaphysical cosmos—for the whole of it. And then they mine that one idea story after story, changing the characters' names and places but generally telling the same story repeatedly.

They don't grow. They stay the same.

They choose to do so because they are interested in something other than self-exploration as a means of expression. They're more interested in self-expression as a means to make an impression. To be a "#1 Bestseller" and be seen as an important figure in the culture by that designation. To be recognized as better than your average bear. And to get rich, too!

And we readers are the ones they are interested in impressing, not as individuals seeking a resolution to an unsolvable problem but as a mass of consumers who run out and buy their bullshit the second it launches on amazon.com!

We don't need any more of those kinds of writers. All we learn from them is how much we aren't like them.

Story Grid requires writers to grow up and become **mythic storytellers** who remind us that we all face difficult choices, and that there is no winning without loss or loss without win.

So what is a story?

It begins with an originating desire.

Whose desire?

The storyteller's desire.

The storyteller's desire for what?

This is the crux of what I'm getting at.

Why are you investing your energy to transform from an aspiring writer into an author? Are you doing so to:

Win an argument?

Prove yourself worthy of attention?

Show off your way with words?

Become the next J.K. Rowling?

Etc.?

These desires will not reveal the truth of what's inside you. And it's my contention that they are **shadow desires**. Writers tell themselves that these are why they want to tell a story.

But the seasoned author knows truth is a much more powerful goal state than "instant bestseller."

The deep desire to write a short story, a novel, or a nonfiction is an internal yearning to share an understanding of a traumatic/euphoric personal experience. And this deep desire is the substance of the fourth holistic transformation.

Here's the thing about traumatic and euphoric experiences. They mirror one another and are inseparable. To experience trauma and to "move forward" despite the allure of surrendering to despair is a triumphant achievement that aids the person who has come through the other side, wounded and scarred but still standing.

To survive a clash with mendacity or contemplation of death is life-altering.

The value attained is immeasurable. Trauma comes in all sizes and kinds of packages, and thus, so do the variational values associated with it.

Euphoria, oddly, can prove traumatic too.

Why does achieving a hard-fought goal and standing at the pinnacle of success prove fleeting? I'd suggest it's because the "winner" has pulled away from the rest of the pack and finds themselves alienated from the ones she's left behind. To win then requires losing connection to friends, family, and tribe. It's not what it's cracked up to be.

"Everything is copy."
— Nora Ephron

Being the center of attention is undoubtedly exciting, but the dark side is that you find yourself alone. Just as trauma alienates the experiencer, threatening their life, their emotional stability, and their sanity, so does euphoria alienate. It's just that the trauma survivor has experienced the direct threat while the euphoric performer experiences a veiled threat.

What's my point here?

The storyteller wishes to explore the trauma and euphoria of their own personal experience, to mine the sorrow or ecstasy of that memory via simulation of another being undergoing a parallel experience. This is an example of what psychologists call the **Solomon effect**, which empowers problem-solving and meaning-making via empathetic dissociation. It's far easier to discover the paradoxical truth of experience if one takes on another's problem, and if the other is an imaginary presence, all the better. Seeing a trauma or triumph from a wider angle proves an effective strategy to find a meaningful resolution. That is, by using the Solomon effect via imaginal pretense, we can take a misunderstanding in our life and transform it into understanding.

This is precisely what Tim Grahl accomplished in his novel *The Shithead*. And I'm pleased to report that many others in our programs are doing the same thing. It's important to note that the works crafted by these other storytellers are absolutely different experiences than Grahl's. They use different genres, and one would be hard-pressed to find their similarities without understanding *The Story Grid Universe* Theory and methodology. What they all are, though, are categories of one.

Unlike a propagandist writer, a story-teller doesn't make an argument. They do not persuade an audience that they are more enlightened. They don't create an artful proof. They generate **novel truth.**

They show and tell the reader that they are not alone, that the world is very discomforting, and that the slings and arrows of circumstance befall us all. There is no privileged vantage point that only a select few can reach where suffering, sacrifice, and death do not touch.

The result of this showing and telling is what Aristotle was getting at with his concept of **catharsis**. Bringing an audience to catharsis brings them to a shared realization of transcendent truth. Being an authentic storyteller capable of poetics and myth-making is all about truth.

Thus, I contend that "writer artists" who narrate from lofty "check me out" perches are, in essence, bullshitters. That doesn't mean they aren't sincere; many, if not most, are heartfelt. They just don't know any better. They have accepted an incorrect paradigm. If I've learned one lesson, it's that the way writing is taught damages the pupil's ability to care for their audience. Thus, the audience is regarded as something to exploit rather than encourage.

As absurd as it sounds, most writers don't consider their audience as other human beings but as a number. They just want a big number, as they believe the more significant the sales of their works, the more they are "measured" as artists. There is far more to life than quantity, namely relationship, quality, and reality.

To desire to be seen, known, and valued; the dream of becoming someone worthy of admiration; to navigate the obstacles and opportunities present; to play finite and infinite games with grace and care for your fellow living and nonliving beings; to problem-solve best bad choices and resolve irreconcilable goods; to perform and behave authentically—these are the truths we at Story Grid endeavor to inch closer to.

Not sales numbers and social currency at all cost. We're not for everyone, and we recognize that as our strength, not our weakness.

"Art invites us to take the journey beyond price, beyond costs into bearing witness to the world as it is and as it should be."

— Toni Morrison

The beauty is that if we get close to attaining our meaningful goals, the sales numbers take care of themselves. Maybe not immediately, but over time, word of mouth is unstoppable, and the mythic stories are the ones that last, not the bullshit ones.

As Martin Luther King put it, "The arc of the moral universe is long, but it bends toward justice." Obviously, there is no justice without truth.

The storyteller tells the truth as best as they can at the moment in their life that they've chosen to represent as universal.

Story Grid's mission is to empower and propagate **authentic narrative truth.** Full stop.

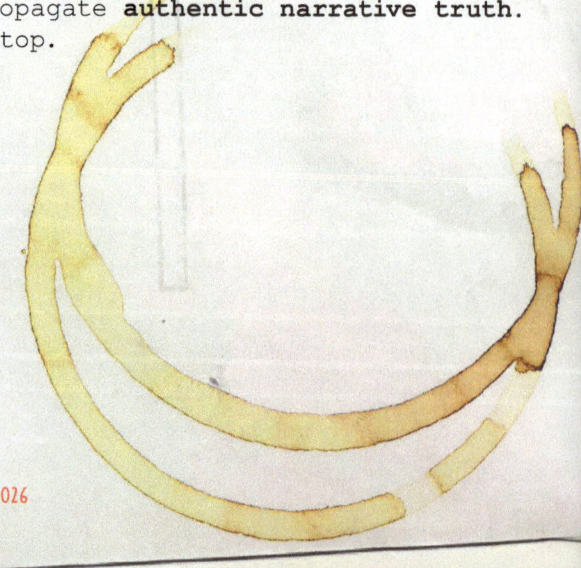

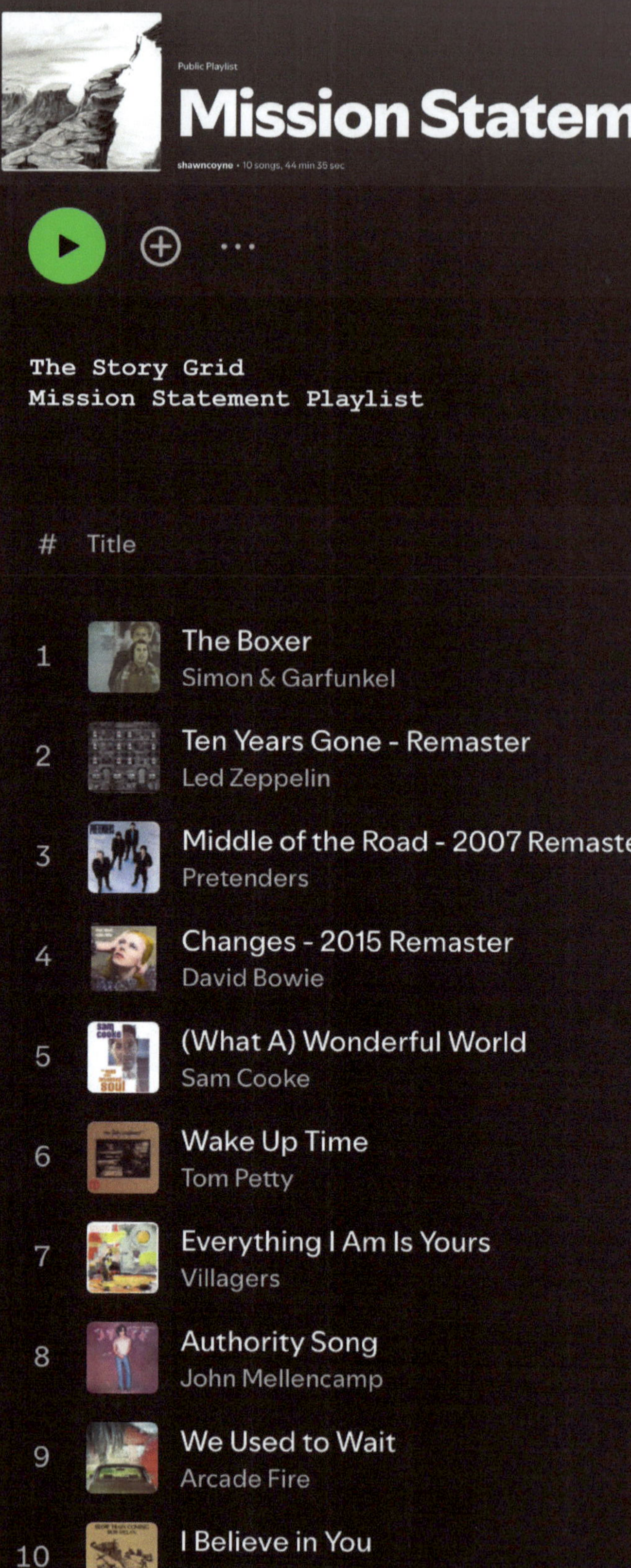

List

Album	
Bridge Over Troubled Water	5:12
Physical Graffiti (Deluxe Edition)	6:34
Learning to Crawl (Expanded & R...	4:14
Hunky Dory (2015 Remaster)	3:37
The Man Who Invented Soul	2:05
Wildflowers	5:19
Darling Arithmetic	3:30
Uh-HUH!	3:49
The Suburbs	5:01
Slow Train Coming	5:10

CONTRIBUTORS

MEETING THE STANDARD

WRITERS

Jeyla Briar, ***Social Studies,*** has been enrolled in our Writer Mentorship Program since July 5, 2025 and lives in Nevada.

Ryan McRae, ***The Candymaker's Son,*** lives in Chicago, Illinois, and has been a student in our Writer Mentorship Program since October 2021.

Sibley Dale, ***Styx,*** has been enrolled in our Writer Mentorship Program since November 8, 2025 and lives in Lille, France.

Brent G. Spalding, ***The Resident Ghost,*** enrolled in our Writer Mentorship Program in 2020. After publishing his first novel ***The Trauma Machine,*** he now works with Story Grid as a mentor in our Writer Mentorship Program. He lives in Mesa, Arizona.

Lark Rowen, ***Guard Rails,*** has been enrolled in our Writer Mentorship Program since September 6, 2025 and lives in Gillingham, England.

Mary Koehler, ***Escalade,*** has been enrolled in our Writer Mentorship Program since November 2024 and lives in Kansas City, Missouri.

W.W. Jacobs, ***The Monkey's Paw,*** **(**1863–1943) was a prolific English author and humorist. ***The Monkey's Paw*** was first published in *Harper's Magazine,* September 1902.

Randall Surles, ***The Game,*** has been working with Story Grid since 2019 and lives in Denton, Texas.

Edith Wharton, ***Xingu*** (1862–1937) was a novelist and short story writer known for her sharp, satirical, and psychologically deep portrayals of Gilded Age New York society. Xingu was first published in *Scribner's Magazine*, December 1911.

Shawn Coyne, ***The Lives We Dream and Do Not Realize,*** is the publisher of *The Standard,* a Story Grid mentor, and the Chief Research and Development Officer of Story Grid. He lives in New York, New York.

EDITORS

Laura Graves, ***Social Studies,*** has been working with Story Grid since 2025 and lives in Texas.

Tim Grahl, ***The Candymaker's Son, The Resident Ghost, The Game,*** and ***The Lives We Dream and Do Not Realize*** is the editor-in-chief of *The Standard,* a Story Grid mentor, and the Chief Executive Officer of Story Grid Universe, LLC., and Story Grid Publishing, LLC. He lives in Nashville, Tennessee.

Krista Adams, ***Styx,*** has been working with Story Grid since 2021 and lives in the Washington, D.C. area.

Kallista Foote, ***Guard Rails,*** has been working with Story Grid since 2023 and lives in Manchester, Tennessee.

Joanne Haines, ***Escalade,*** has been working with Story Grid since 2023 and lives in Anchorage, Alaska.

Henry Mills Alden, ***The Monkey's Paw,*** (1836–1919) was an American author and editor for *Harper's magazine* for fifty years. He was a key figure in American literature during the late 19th and early 20th centuries.

Edward L. Burlingame, ***Xingu,*** (1848–1922) was the founding editor-in-chief of *Scribner's Magazine* (1886–1914). He was an American writer and editor and on the editorial staff of the *New York Tribune* in 1871. He was born in Boston, Massachusetts but lived in New York City.

ARTISTS

Victor Juhasz created the artwork for the cover image, *The Lives We Dream and Do Not Realize,* and the staff illustrations. He lives in upstate New York and can be contacted at https://juhaszillustration.com

Sasha Davydova created the artwork for *Social Studies, Guard Rails,* and *The Candymaker's Son.* She lives in New York, New York, and can be contacted via Instagram @sashatattoo.nyc.

Timothy Hsu contributed artwork for *The Candymaker's Son.* He lives in New York and can be contacted via chinatownsoup.nyc.

Clare Kim created the artwork for *Resident Ghost* and The Story Grid Universe advertising page. She lives in Brooklyn, New York, and can be contacted via clarekim.com.

Layne Miller contributed artwork for *Styx.* He lives in Long Island, New York, and can be contacted via layne-miller.com.

Sonnie Kozlover contributed artwork for *Guard Rails.* She lives in Brooklyn, New York and can be contacted via chinatownsoup.nyc.

Boy Kong lives in Orlando, Florida, and can be contacted via chinatownsoup.nyc.

Kimmy Quillin contributed artwork for *The Game.* She lives in Brooklyn, New York, and can be contacted via chinatownsoup.nyc.

HUNTER created the artwork for *Xingu* and *The Monkey's Paw.* He lives in New York, New York and can be contacted via hunterkeene.com.

Victor Castro contributed photography to *The Lives We Dream and Do Not Realize.* He lives in Bronx, New York, and can be contacted via hivictorcastro.mypixieset.com.

Masa Shigeta contributed artwork for *The Lives We Dream and Do Not Realize.* He lives in New Jersey and can be contacted via chinatownsoup.nyc.

FOUNDERS

SETTING THE STANDARD

AL MUSITANO
BRENT G. SPALDING
PASCAL A. KIRCHNER
MICHAEL WALSH
BOLEN GADDY
KATHERINE LYNN LEUBA
JULIA BLAIR
KRISTA K. ADAMS
DEBRA W. KINCHELOE
GERARD REBAGLIATI
LINDA A. SMITH
BILLY HARTWIG
RUSSELL BROTHERS
ANONYMOUS
KAYLA DAVENPORT BOOKS
RODNEY DEATON, MD, JD
DARYL SPIRKA
DAVID A VOGEL JR
THADDEUS A. PODBIELSKI
GAIL BRENNER NASTASIA
D. SCOTT THAYER
K ALLEN BAKER
HOLLY MARSH PERRINO
CHRIS OVERSON
BRIAN L. McCALEB
ANONYMOUS

ANDY KURNIA
MARC RODRIGUES-BERNET
A NONY MOUSE
VALERIE HENRY
LAURA MACKENZIE
JUSTIN ROBINSON
MICHAEL McCLELLAN
MICHAEL De La MAZA
KRISTI STALDER
JOHN AND AMY SCANLAN
ORAN MAGAL
DANA OLIVER
ANONYMOUS
CLAUDETTE JOHNSON
KATE WOOD
JOHNE COOK
GEORGE J KOURY
MICHELLE GLASSLEY
SCOTT C. MITCHELL
SARAH KATHERINE
McASHAN
JANE DONALDSON, Toronto, On
WILLIAM BABB
ELLEN M. McCURDY
C SHATZEL
ALICIA JEAN

DEMETROPOLIS
KARLA M. DIAZ PERERA
DAVE MUMA
CLINTON De YOUNG
KALLISTA FOOTE
RYAN McRAE
ANDREA MURSCHEL
JAN BOWLER
ANONYMOUS
PAYSON F. COOPER
ALI KASPER
KEVIN R. WORTHLEY
TIM GRAHL, SR.
KAREN GRAHL
MAX GRAHL
CONNOR GRAHL
CANDACE GRAHL
TIM GRAHL
CROSBY COYNE
WAVERLY COYNE
BLEECKER COYNE
BIBB BAILEY
SHAWN COYNE

1. Security Breach

2. Getting the Message

3. Close Call

4. Enlistment

5. Leaving Home

6. Unexpected Outcome

7. Grappling with Trust

8. Crossroads Challenge

9. Epiphany

10. No Turning Back

11. Radical Demand

12. Gut Check

13. The Abyss

14. Defection

15. Coming Back

16. Showdown

17. Giving the Message

18. The Pinnacle

19. Revelation

20. A New Home

SEE THE FOREST

Twenty True Scenes. The myth reveals.

The Story Grid Guild Program

Progressive Self-Discovery of Hidden Masterwork Craft

Volume 1 / Number 1 2026

www.ingramcontent.com/pod-product-compliance
Lightning Source LLC
LaVergne TN
LVHW070130110826
845147LV00002B/225